STORIES YOU CAN SING ALONG TO!

BY
JOE CUNNINGHAM
ARTWORK BY
MIKE JOHANNSEN

Table of Contents

This book is dedicated to all of the family, friends, co-workers & random people who supported and encouraged us along the way.

Lung Butter

The alarm clock went off and Harvey Carson woke up feeling like a gorilla had sat on his chest. He'd had the slightest scratch in his throat when he'd gone to sleep. He'd known he was coming down with something. What had settled in his chest overnight was worse than anything he'd ever felt before. He sat up in bed and found it even more difficult to breathe. He reached over to the alarm clock and cut off CCR's "Bad Moon Rising" mid-song. He coughed gingerly and his lungs felt like they were on fire. He tried to clear his throat but that set off a chest spasm that rocked him to the core of his being. Towards the end of the coughing fit he felt something dislodge inside and enter his mouth. He leapt out of bed and ran to the bathroom. He grabbed the sides of the sink and unleashed a greenish-yellow loogie about the size of a Ping-Pong ball. It hit the bottom of the sink with a meaty "THWACK!", a single rivulet of clear saliva running down the drain while the rest stayed put. Harvey gave the phlegm globber a look of revulsion, then peered at it closer. Mixed in with the already distinguishable colors were flecks of grey (no doubt from his years as a smoker) and tiny strands of red that he could only assume were blood. He began to cough again and spat up another mouthful of phlegm identical to its brother in the sink, only slightly larger.

Now that he was fully awake, Harvey could feel his head pounding and his sinuses were clogged. He knew then he wasn't going to work. It would be the first time since he started at the power plant that he'd called in. He dialed up his boss and, before he could even get a complete sentence out, his boss gave him the next two days off. Harvey hung up the phone and went back to the bathroom to hack another chest-burster in to the sink, this one larger than the other two combined. He turned on the water to wash down the phlegm, but they were stubborn at first and didn't want to relinquish their hold on the porcelain. Harvey increased the flow of water and finally all three globs went down the drain. Harvey could now feel the fever gripping him and returned to his bed. He lay there a few minutes, but his heaving chest would not let him get comfortable. He went to his medicine cabinet to see if he had any dextromethorphan and found a few packets of Thera-Flu. He took them to the kitchen and followed the instructions on the packet, doubling it to make it stronger. He drank down the warm liquid when it was assembled and it felt great on his throat. He returned to the bathroom and had another coughing fit, unleashing the biggest wad yet. When he spat it into the sink, it quivered like a mini Jell-O mold for a few seconds then stopped. Curiously Harvey poked it with a finger and it quivered again. Harvey then washed it as well down the sink. He cleared his throat again, relieved that nothing came up this time, and took to his bed once more. He had a box of Kleenex on his nightstand next to the bed; he took a couple and blew his nose. He opened the tissues up to see what his nostrils and sinuses had produced, but it was only clear snot. Nothing like the colorful gems he'd spat out in the sink. He deposited the tissues in to the wastebasket next to the night-stand and pulled the covers up close to his chin. The medicine was beginning to take

8

effect and he began to feel drowsy. He closed his eyes and felt himself drifting off, but then the DM kicked in and he felt another fit coming on. He peeled back the covers and raced to the sink just in time to expel a nasty lunger that hit the sink basin and spread out into a rough Africa looking shape. It quivered like the last offering to the sink, but when Harvey turned the water on to wash it down, it seemed to move away from the stream and drain. It moved towards Harvey, in fact. He pulled the stopper on the sink, let the basin fill up some; eventually the glob of phlegm was floating in the water. He released the stopper to drain the sink and the water took the glob with it. Harvey thought for a minute about the way it seemed to move toward him, but then chalked it up to a side effect of the medication. His throat was burning again, so he filled a glass with water and gulped it down. It soothed the burn somewhat, but not totally. He went back to bed and this time he did fall asleep.

Harvey woke up about two hours later, according to the alarm clock next to the Kleenex on the night-stand. It now felt like a hippo, rather than a gorilla, had taken up residence astride him. He struggled to sit up and swung his legs over the edge of the bed, putting his feet gingerly on the floor. He raised his head and began a series of whooping, hacking coughs that finally dislodged a huge chunk of something. It flew out of Harvey's mouth at the end of one of these hacks like a cat issuing forth a hairball with little warning and splatted on the floor between him and the bathroom. The trajectory of the globule and the force with which it impacted the floor made it resemble a teardrop shape. It had the same color and texture as the others that had found their home and demise in the sink, but was far larger than the rest. Harvey grimaced at the sight of it and vowed to go to the hospital. This was no illness that Thera-Flu was going to knock out. He rose from bed to clean up the phlegm first and stepped over it to get to the bathroom for a decent sized wad of toilet paper. He came back with the paper and bent over to wipe up his projectile. As he reached towards it, it seemed to shrink back away from him. He stood up, frowned and looked at the glob on the floor. No, it was still in the same shape as it was when it left his face and landed on the ground. He bent over again and quickly wiped the glob off the floor,

9

turned and entered the bathroom shaking it out of the paper into the sink. It smacked the porcelain and hung fast. Harvey turned on the water full blast and put his thumb under the faucet to aim the stream at the glob to dislodge it from the sink. It did the trick and the glob was quickly flushed down the drain to join its brethren. Harvey left the water running and splashed some on his face, then cupped his hands and drank some. He raised his red-rimmed eyes to the mirror and inspected his face. Nothing was amiss. He turned off the faucet and was turning to leave the bathroom when he heard a gurgling coming from the drain. He paused with his hand on the light switch, looking back over his shoulder to the sink. There was water rising up from the drain. Harvey grumbled and grabbed the plunger from beside the toilet. He turned the water back on and filled it some, then stuck the plunger in and gave it a few pumps. He retracted the plunger and the water went immediately back down. Satisfied, he returned the plunger to its place and went to make ready for a trip to the E.R. He shuffled to his closet and got out a flannel and a pair of jeans, putting them on after removing his nightclothes. Next he shuffled to the dresser and selected a pair of socks, taking care to ensure they matched. After that were work boots, which, along with the pair of sandals he had, were the only footwear he owned. Finally, he donned a Red Sox baseball cap and went to the nightstand to get his keys. As he was reaching for them, he heard the gurgling sound coming from the bathroom sink again. He looked at it quizzically and went across the room, entering the bathroom and turning on the light. Harvey expected to see water in the basin again and froze when he saw it was decidedly not. What filled the basin was what appeared to be every bit of phlegm he had ever spat into that sink, since there was much more of it than what he had contributed that day. It was colored exactly like his expectorant from the day. It writhed and pulsed in the sink, seemingly alive and breathing. Harvey made a repulsed and shocked sound thick with the mucus that was still in his chest. The phlegm globber pulsed excitedly in his direction, reaching out for him with a snotty tendril. Harvey backed up against the bathroom doorjamb and stared in to the sink. The glob pulsed again in his direction and then, with a heave, sloshed itself out of the sink and on to the floor a few feet away from him. Harvey backed up out of the room in horror, his feet becoming tangled together. He went down in a heap and smacked his head on the floor, dazing himself. His eyes rolled around in his head for a couple of seconds then regained focus. He stared ahead at the bathroom floor and saw the glob had left that room and joined him in this one. Still dazed from the fall, Harvey sat up. That was as far as he got. The phlegm glob launched itself at Harvey's face and stuck to the lower half of it, with some of it entering Harvey's gaping, surprised mouth. It started to spread out and cover the rest of his face, entering his nostrils and wrapping around towards his ears. He could feel it sliding down his throat and re-entering the lungs that had discharged it hours ago, entering the corners of his eyes and seeping in to his brain. Harvey tried to scream but his mouth and throat, along with every other orifice in his head, was plugged.

The Protector

The police finished getting the description from the guy in the Nissan. He stated that the man in the van had been parked across the street. The two little girls had only been missing for about two hours. The parents had called the cops in the first half hour of the abduction when they hadn't returned from the bodega they were going to for ice cream. If the cops could get a BOLO out with an accurate take on the perp, they might be able to track him before he got too far. From what Nissan Guy said, the two girls were walking down the sidewalk when the dirty van screeched to a halt next to them and the guy hucked them into the back of the van, which he padlocked from the outside. He scrambled around to the driver's side, jumped in and peeled out of there. There were excellent tire patterns for CSU to look at, analyze and match to the van, but that was court case stuff. Monohan had to try to get the actual guy by relying on wits, intuition and gut. The science would be there to nail the guy in court once he was caught. The van had been north bound and Nissan Guy said when it got to Schaefer Avenue, it turned right and went east towards the Warehouse District. Monohan hoped that was the perp's destination: an abandoned warehouse with a stash spot where he meant to do those girls harm. Monohan was not going to let that happen. They established the BOLO with the van and perp's description, but Monohan wanted to go directly to the Warehouse District. He rounded up a couple of plainclothes and headed in that direction. With the two hour head-start there was no telling which one he might have gone in, but Monohan hoped that maybe he was in such a hurry to get to his prize that he left the van outside the warehouse. That would just be dumb luck. Monohan would have to follow his gut, try to see through the perp's mind's eye, to think like him. They arrived at the Warehouse District within fifteen minutes. Most of the active warehouses were situated up front. All the abandoned or un-leased ones were located in the center and the rear. Monohan guessed the perp would be squatting in one of the abandoned warehouses. No way would he take the chance to lease one, much less squat in one that was still on the market and could have prospective renters dropping by at any time. No, this guy would need quiet and solitude to do his evil business. An abandoned warehouse would suit those needs quite nicely. Monohan had already received a list of the abandoned ones while en route to the district, so he had a good idea of where to start. There were four grouped together that were all abandoned, it had to be one of those. Monohan directed the plainclothes to fan out, look for anything suspicious and if anything was found to report to him immediately, while he set his sights on the warehouse that was furthest away from any and all activity. He proceeded in that direction, flashlight out and gun holstered but at the ready. His warehouse was of course dark, but that didn't mean that it was devoid of any activity. He reached the corner of the building and put his back to the wall, straining to hear any sounds that might emit. There was no van in his line of sight, so he walked the length of the wall to the backside of the building and peered around the corner. This perp was either very brave or very stupid, for as Monohan rounded the corner of the building, there stood the van, padlock hanging from the back door, unlocked. They had to be inside.

Monohan crept toward the van and looked inside the windows, but it was empty. There was a single door on the rear wall of the warehouse, Monohan made his way there carefully and tested the knob to the windowless door. Unbelievably, it was unlocked and he cracked it open enough to peer inside into more darkness. He swung the door open and slipped inside. At this point he withdrew his weapon from the holster and swept the room with his flashlight. The warehouse was empty, save for an office type room against the right wall. Light emitted from the room but no sound. Monohan hoped that the lack of sound wasn't a bad sign; that the perp had already done his evil and was contemplating his next move or something. He stayed close to the wall and made his way around the room towards the office. As he got closer, he could finally hear some murmuring as well as light music playing. He was able to identify it as "In The Air Tonight" by Phil Collins. Monohan crept as close to the office as he dared and was able to distinct a male voice, soothing in tone and not at all what he expected. He was finally able to make out words but not complete sentences. He couldn't tell if the perp was talking to live or dead subjects, but either way he was speaking softly to them. The office was the size of a small apartment with two windows flanking a front door and another window on the wall that Monohan was creeping ever toward. All of the windows had blinds drawn, but he was sure he could survey the room through one of the little holes in the blinds where the drawstrings were threaded through. Now, as he peered through one of the little slits, not only could he see the perp, but was able to make out some of what he was saying to whomever he was addressing.

"...I will get you through this night, and then I will decide what to do about your parents." The Perp said. Monohan stiffened, was this guy going after entire families? So many questions started swirling in his head, he had to tamp them down and focus on getting the girls out of here. There would be time for these questions later. Phil Collins was replaced by Sarah McLachlan's "Angel" and Monohan rounded the corner of the office. He was now at the front underneath one of the two windows. He looked through the slits and now saw that the room was occupied by The Perp and two, very much alive, little girls. He had neither bound nor gagged them. They sat together on what appeared to be a rollaway cot and both were holding orange sodas with squiggly straws in them. They were also both fully dressed and appeared unharmed in any way, which he found unusual indeed. The Perp had had these girls for more than two hours now, and had yet to do anything with them. Monohan looked back to The Perp and sized him up: he appeared to be unarmed and very calm, even though he was pacing back and forth. He was sure that with the element of surprise on his side he could take this guy. There might not be any need to bring in the plainclothes that were outside. Monohan gripped his weapon and inched away from the window to reposition himself in front of the door. Meaning to kick it in, maybe The Perp would be near enough to be caught by it swinging open and add to the surprise. The music changed once again, now it was "Wait" by M83. Monohan steeled himself and got his pistol at the ready. He did an internal countdown from three to zero and at zero he kicked in the door with as much force as he could muster. As luck would have it, The Perp was right behind the door as it flew open, catching him flush in the face and knocking him to the floor in a daze. Monohan rushed in to the room and leveled his pistol at The Perp while shining the flashlight in his eyes.

"Freeze, shit-head!!" he exclaimed. The Perp was gathering himself and shaking his head as if to free the cobwebs, but did not make a move to get off the floor. He looked up at Monohan, bleeding from a cut in his forehead and a split lip. His mouth moved as if to say something but no sound came out. His eyes locked with Monahan's and finally he was able to say something.

"Please, you don't understand, let me ex-..."

"Shut up, asshole! I said freeze, and that means your mouth, too!" Very quickly, Monohan cast a sideways glance at the girls then his gaze was back on The Perp.

"What makes you think you were going to get away with this? Snatching two little girls off the street like that?"

"I wasn't trying to get away with anything, officer, if you'd just let me explain," The Perp pleaded. The song on the stereo changed to "Sunshine on my Shoulders" by John Denver. This guy had weird taste in music, Monohan noted.

"You can explain all you want down at the station, numb-nuts. Get off the floor and keep your hands up." The Perp rose slowly, steadying himself against the wall. He appeared to be a bit groggy still from the door introducing itself to his face. He raised his hands as requested, but continued to speak.

"Really, I have an explanation for all of this that we can discuss right here, no need to go anywhere."

"Hmmph," Monohan grunted. "Nothing you have to say will change what you have done here. You took two innocent, little girls off the street, away from their families and that's all the explanation I need. Now turn around, face the wall and place your palms against it." The Perp made no move to comply, just continued his pleading with Monohan.

"Officer, please. You're making a big mistake. If you'd just let me show you what I have here in my pocket…" The Perp made a move to reach inside his jacket and that's when Monohan shot him. The Perp went down in a heap, blood gushing from the wound, indicating that he was alive and still had a pulse. Monohan rushed over to The Perp and quickly handcuffed him, should the wound prove to be non-lethal and The Perp decided he still had some fight left in him. Monohan radioed to the plainclothes who were already on their way, having heard the shot ring out. They summoned a bus to collect the wounded Perp and deliver him to a hospital, hopefully to keep him alive so he could answer for his crimes. Monohan turned his attention to the girls as the plainclothes attended to The Perp.

"You girls alright?" he asked.

"Yessir," they answered in unison, still holding their orange sodas.

"I'll need you to put those sodas down so they can be collected as evidence and make sure they're not drugged or anything, OK?" They did as they were asked and placed the drinks on the table next to the stereo, which was now playing "When the Man Comes Around" by Johnny Cash. Monohan switched it off as Mr. Cash was singing about hearing the trumpets and the pipers.

"OK, ladies, we're going to get you home to both of your families as soon as possible. How does that sound?" he asked with a smile. Neither girl answered, but both nodded vigorously as a reply. More cops had begun to show up at the scene, as well as the ambulance to take The Perp to the hospital. Monohan began to feel the swelling of pride that comes with a job well done; the girls would be going home safe and sound, The Perp (if he lived) would stand trial for his crimes. Even though he had acted alone and went cowboy on the situation, he was sure he would get praise heaped on him from not only two grateful families, but his department as well. It was a good shooting according to IAB. Even though it was determined The Perp had no weapon, Monohan still acted correctly given the situation. He would be allowed to personally deliver the girls back to their families and then it would be paperwork for the rest of the night. The only thing The Perp had inside of his jacket was a small spiral notepad filled with all kinds of rambling and gibberish, and a talisman of some sort on a silver chain. The Perp could try to explain all of this stuff if, and when, he woke up. Right now it was time to get these girls home before the clock rolled over to midnight and the start of a new day began. He loaded the girls up in his car and only had to drive to one home. Both families were at one residence keeping vigil and now that they had been found, awaiting their girls' return. Monohan drove up the driveway of the house, a tidy little ranch house not too far from where the girls were originally taken from. Both sets of parents were waiting at the doorstep as Monohan drove up, but they did not approach the car. Instead, Monohan pulled the car to a stop and let the girls out, whereupon they ran to the house and their awaiting parents. Both of the mothers present ushered the girls inside as the fathers stood to greet Monohan as he approached. Both men held their hands out to him to shake and began to thank him for returning their girls safe and sound. That's when Monohan's radio began to crackle with life in his car.

"Detective Monohan. Respond please. Over." Monohan apologized to the two men and asked to be excused for a moment. He returned to his car and leaned inside to grab the radio.

"This is Monohan. Go ahead. Over."

"Detective, if you haven't made it to the residence, you are requested to turn around and deliver the girls to the station immediately. Over."

"Sorry dispatch, but I'm already here and the girls are safe inside, probably preparing for bed as we speak. What's this all about, anyway? Over."

"Chief says The Perp woke up in the ambulance and started spouting off a lot of crazy stuff. Chief wants you to bring the girls to the station so we can sort all of this out. Over."

"OK. Give me a few minutes. I'll get the girls loaded up and bring them that way. Does he want the parents to accompany? Over."

"No, Detective, just the girls and as soon as possible. Over." Monohan dropped the radio and turned to face the fathers to make his request. That's when the world went black.

Monohan blinked awake, head pounding and vision blurry. He was lying next to his car and could hear his radio squawking at him from the front seat.

"DETECTIVE MONOHAN!! COME IN DETECTIVE MONOHAN!!"

He struggled to gain his footing and leaned into the car to grab the radio.

"Monohan here," he slurred.

"Detective, what is your status? Where are the girls? Are you en route? Over." Monohan looked towards the house. It was dark and the front door was wide open.

"Negative dispatch, I am not en route and I think I was assaulted. Over." Monohan felt about his head and winced when he came to a tender spot on the front, just above his brow. He looked again towards the house with its open door.

"Detective, more officers are en route to your location. Stay put and wait for their arrival. Is that clear? Over."

"Got it," Monohan said, already dropping the radio in the front seat and un-holstering his weapon for the second time that night. He walked toward the house and its open front door, entering the darkness within. He was immediately hit with the smell of decomposition, strong enough to make him gag and take a step back. How had he not smelled this before when he first dropped the girls off? He pulled his tie to his nose to stifle the smell then went further inside, flipping on the first light switch he came across. It was a slaughterhouse: two goats were nailed to the wall in an upside-down crucifixion pose, slit from neck to anus, their entrails piled on the ground below them. Strange symbols were written on the walls in a dark maroon substance (presumably blood from the goats) and between the goat's entrails on the floor were a single snuffed out black candle. Monohan penetrated deeper into the house, turning on lights as he went. Each room had the strange symbol markings as the walls in the main room. He was almost done sweeping the house when he heard the first patrol car pull up. He went to the front of the house to greet the newly arrived cops.

"Detective! What's your status?" the first patrolman inquired.

"I'm hurt, I'm pissed, and I want to know what the hell is going on here!" he spat back at the officer. More cars pulled up, including the Chiefs.

"At ease, Monohan!" Chief Mercer barked at him. "You were told to not enter the residence. What part of that was unclear?"

"Sorry, Chief, but with all due respect, you weren't the one who got knocked the fuck out, and I wanted to find the son of a bitch who did it to me. What is going on here?"

"It's a big fucking shit sandwich is what it is and we're all nibbling on it. That guy you took down earlier, did he say anything to you?"

"He kept trying to plead his case, saying it was all a misunderstanding or something. You know, perp talk. He went for what I thought was a weapon and I put him down. What's he got to do with this?"

"His name is Father Jacob Whitier. When he woke up in the bus he started screaming about Satanists and the little girls and that he had to protect them. Of course we figured him to be a raving lunatic at this point, but he collected himself long enough to explain the book and talisman in his possession. He apparently took the girls not to harm them, but to protect them from the people who did this mess here. Same ones that conked you on the head, as well."

"Satanists?" Monohan was incredulous. "What is this, some cheeseball horror movie?"

"Afraid not, Detective," Chief Mercer replied. "Whitier says those two little girls are to be human sacrifices used in a ritual to bring about the end of days at Satan's hands. He's been watching them for weeks, waiting for them to let their guard down long enough to snatch up the girls and secure them away. His guess is that they let them go to the bodega to get one last treat. You were just too good at your job and found him before he could change locations. The warehouse was his first stop, to try to calm the girls and bring them around to what was going to happen to them and how he was there to protect them. It appears you interrupted that, which is why the girls were so willing to get back to their parents."

"So, those people I delivered the girls to are actually their parents and they are going to kill their own children?"

"It would appear so, Detective. The only consolation we can take, according to Father Whitier, is that it is after midnight, and they can't complete their ritual now, mostly thanks in part to the good Father for his actions, but in part to you, too, for delaying them with your forehead."

"I need to talk to this Whitier, I have to save those girls." Monohan tried to push past Mercer, but Mercer gripped him firmly around the bicep.

"Soon, Monohan. You can talk to the Father, we can get this sorted out and figure out where to go next. Whitier says we have time, anyway. They can't attempt another ritual for ninety days, based on some mumbo-jumbo that I don't understand. But that's what matters, Detective. We have time. You can talk to Whitier *and* do your job *and* find those girls soon, but first you need to get that lump on your head checked out."

200 A.Z.

The old lady shambled down the street in her old lady dress, her slippers still attached to her feet. As she neared the intersection, her head exploded like a watermelon tossed off of a high-rise.

"HAHA!" Sanchez exclaimed. "I never get tired of doing that!" Marcos "Dirty" Sanchez was a twenty-one year old shelf stocker at Wal-Mart before the outbreak, but now he was the south sentry for our little makeshift army/family. He was the best sniper in the group, with the bulk of his training coming at the hands of Call of Duty: Black Ops. He took to the real thing like a fish to water and to date had the most snuffs out of all of us. There were twenty of us in all, but most of us weren't fighters, just survivors. Sure, most of us had or could take out a chud if necessary, that was why we were here in the first place. Once here, it was clear that there were those that would do the bulk of the fighting, while the rest of us worked on surviving. I was a survivor, but I had two chud snuffs under my belt: Joey Padalecki, the neighbor kid, and Harry Kramer, my step-dad.

I woke up to a world in chaos. The morning of the outbreak, Joey had attacked my mom first, killing her instead of turning her while Harry got bit in the attack trying to defend her. I had run to the backyard when I heard the screams. Brandishing a baseball bat, I made a home run swing that connected with the base of Joey's skull and sent his head flopping forward, no longer connected to its spine. I didn't know how long Harry had left. I had seen enough zombie movies to know that he was doomed, and he knew it too. He told me that he didn't want to eat me, or anybody for that matter, and for me to do the right thing. So I caved in the front of his skull with the bat. So maybe he wasn't technically a chud yet, but he would have been soon, so I say it still counts. I dropped the bat there; I didn't want to use it anymore. That was when I met the first of our group as she came bounding over the fence. Hilary Beasley, formerly of the Johnson Street Beasley's, a family known in the area as having a rough edge. She was a fighter, and very attractive even under the considerable amounts of gore she was drenched in.

"You bit?" she asked.

"No," I replied. I looked her up and down. I'm sure her outfit was quite smashing before some of the townspeople shed their blood on it. She was carrying a machete and had a revolver stuffed in her waistband.

"You're the first person I've come across, Ortega," she said. "If we stick together, we just might make it out of this."

"Where's the rest of your family?" I asked.

"On my shirt," she replied. We went back inside my house and she threw some stuff in the backpack she was carrying and I went to look for a more suitable weapon. I finally settled on a pair of garden shears.

"What are you going to do with those, give 'em haircuts?" she asked. I snipped the air a couple of times to show I meant business. She just laughed at me and reached in to her bag. She withdrew another revolver, identical to the one in her waistband.

"Here, it was my dad's," she said as she handed it to me, followed by a handful of bullets. "Just pop it open right there and empty the spent shells to reload it, and try not to shoot me." I had only handled plastic guns before, but those instructions seemed simple enough. I stuffed the gun into my own waistband and asked her what our next move was.

"Get to high ground. These things aren't very good climbers. Also try to find more survivors, safety in numbers is where it's at. Besides, the more people in the group, the better your odds are of not getting bit." She went to the sink and washed her hands and face then dried them with a towel hung from the oven handle.

"Hey, that's not a dish towel!" I blurted out. She looked at me incredulously.

"Does it really fucking matter?" she asked impatiently. Remembering my dead mother in the back yard, I told her that I supposed it didn't at this point.

We left my house behind with Hilary in the lead and me covering her rear...um, I mean our rear. Her plan was to go to the church. Not because she wanted to pray, but she figured that's where a bunch of people would have gathered seeking shelter from this flesh eating storm. She was half right. A bunch of people had gathered there, but Father O' Malley had begun to eat them, so they were all running in different, screaming directions. Most of them were promptly beset upon by the boys' choir that Father O' Malley had been conducting at the time of the outbreak. One guy made it out and was running right for us. Hilary leveled her gun at him, but he made no move to stop his forward progress.

"HOLY FUCKING SHIT HELP ME!!!" he screamed at us.

"YOU BIT?" Hilary yelled back.

"GOD NO!! I threw Widow Perkins at one that was trying to get me and it got her instead. Old bat had it coming anyway." He had come to a halt between us and was trying to get his breath back.

"We have to move," Hilary said. "Plan B."

"You didn't tell me what 'Plan B' was," I said.

"I'm still thinking of it, give me a sec," she said. Screaming Guy was looking around wildly, eyes bugging out of his head.

"Anybody got a spare weapon?" he asked.

"Nope," Hilary said and began to move towards the Wal-Mart.

"Plan B?" I asked.

28

"Yep," she replied. "Stay in the middle of us, Jethro." She apparently knew Screaming Guy, and his name was Jethro. We walked briskly through the church parking lot and crossed the street to the Wal-Mart. We had made it halfway across the lot and had to round an eighteen wheeler to get a clear look at the front door. We came around the back end and, as we breached the corner, a chud lurched out and grabbed at Hilary. She was struggling with it and trying to get at her gun at the same time, but then suddenly she didn't have to, as the chud's head exploded and it slumped to the ground. Hilary was going to have to wash her face again. We heard a triumphant hoot from the Wal-Mart and then a long whistle. We looked towards the store and saw a brown man on the roof waving his hands at us.

"It's all clear!" he yelled. "Make your way to the front door!" We did as he suggested double time. We got to the stores doors and saw more people behind them. They removed their makeshift blockade and let us in. The brown guy from the roof was making his way toward us, grinning from ear to ear. That's how we met "Dirty" Sanchez.

All in all, there were eleven other people in the store, not counting Sanchez and our trio. That brought it to fifteen. We learned that Sanchez was an employee, along with three other people, and the rest were just customers. There were no kids in the group, but there was an elderly couple who would probably slow us down if we had to break out of here as a group. Sanchez introduced us to the rest: his fellow employees were Jeff Clark, Katie Reed and Jill Wheatley. They were all a part of the night stocking crew and all about the same age. The customers were the elderly couple, Stan and Edith Gunkle, Chip Younger, a cook from out of town, Steve and Craig, a gay black couple who seemed attached at the hip, Bernie

Little, a well-known shyster around town, and Bob and Bill McMullen, the local ne'er-do-wells. After introductions had been made, the McMullen brothers went to hunt for a buzz, bypassing the beer aisle and heading straight for the pharmacy. One of the two, I couldn't tell which, was whistling a tune that sounded very similar to "Short Change Hero" by The Heavy. Hilary rounded everybody else up and started to map out a plan; if this group was lacking a leader, they had one now.

"We can't stay here, so everyone round up a backpack, load it with essentials and grab whatever weapons you're comfortable carrying and/or know how to use. I don't want to get shot in the back because one of you can't handle a shotgun properly."

"I don't understand why we can't stay here," Stan Gunkle spoke up. "There's plenty of food and beverages, enough weapons to arm ourselves as well as a decent number of people to make a stand with."

"We can't stay here because a) we're at ground level and b) there are too many entrances to cover and not enough people. We need to get to an apartment building or something with several floors. We need to be on higher ground, and before you say it, that doesn't mean the roof of this building is adequate." Stan closed his mouth, it seemed that was what he was about to say. I noticed Jethro heading towards the pharmacy to join the McMullen brothers; hopefully he'd be smart enough to grab first aid gear while he was back there. The rest of us retreated into the store to gather the supplies we needed and add to our arsenal.

We reconvened at the front of the store about forty-five minutes later to work out the next part of our plan. Even the McMullen boys and Jethro were there, albeit high as kites.

"I'm a supersonic, goddamn force of nature!" Jethro crowed and the McMullens laughed behind him.

"Shut up, Jethro," Hilary said, and he did so. "OK, we've got two choices, The Firestone Building two blocks from here or The King's Arms Apartments."

"Where's the King's Arms?" Chip Younger asked.

"Around the Queens ass!" Jethro hooted, followed by more raucous laughter from the McMullens. Hilary just rolled her eyes and otherwise ignored Jethro.

"It's about four blocks east, but it's taller than the Firestone. I know a few people that live there, so we may not need to break in to it," she said to Younger. "The Firestone may be harder to get in, but it's closer."

"So it's basically fifty-fifty on the both of them?" Younger asked.

"Essentially, yes. Personally, I feel better about the King's Arms," Hilary said. Jethro snickered but said nothing. Steve and Craig, who had been silent up to this point, voiced their support of Hilary's choice to go to the King's Arms.

"We know some people in that building, too. A couple of queens we do costumes for," Steve said.

"Yeah, bitches still owe us money for their last show, they better let us in," Craig chimed in.

"Well, that increases our odds of getting in slightly," Hilary said. "Anybody else know someone in that building?"

"Jill knows a guy, but she only talks to him online," Katie Reed said. Jill poked her in the ribs.

"He's shy, very introverted," she explained. Her face had turned crimson.

"Bullshit," Jeff Clark said. "He's a nut-bag who probably sits naked in front of his computer waiting for you to pop online then he strokes his johnson with steel wool while he talks to you. All while giving himself a peanut butter enema." There seemed to be a hint of jealousy in Jeff's voice.

"Well, it doesn't matter who he is or what he's doing with his peanut butter. If he can help get us in the building, then that's a plus in my book," Hilary said. "Then it's decided. The King's Arms it is."

The first three blocks of our journey to The King's Arms were uneventful. We could see chuds everywhere, but they didn't come at us. They all seemed to be preoccupied with the chewing on of body parts. Once we got to the corner of the fourth block, though, Hilary held up a hand to halt our progress then motioned for us to retreat. We retraced our steps and ducked into an alley.

"There's a pack of them smack dab in front of the building," she said. We all looked at each other, struggling for ideas of what to do next. That was when I noticed that Bernie Little wasn't there anymore.

"Hey, Hilary," I said, "the ambulance chaser is gone."

"He was bringing up the rear; he must have dropped off at some point." She told us to stay put, she was going to go assess the situation in front of the building we were attempting to get in to. She came back a few minutes later, shaking her head but smiling.

"What's up?" I asked.

"I found the lawyer," she said, "unfortunately for him, so did they."

"What the hell was he thinking?"

"I think he lives in the building and just used us to get here safely. Bastard tried to leave us behind and get himself in. Apparently he tripped trying to make it to the front of the building and they were on him. Dumb son of a bitch dropped his keys, too," Hilary said, holding up the newly acquired keys for all to see. We celebrated quietly; we now had our way into the building.

The first floor of the building contained the leasing office, laundry room and mail center. All of the apartments were on the second floor and above. We did a quick sweep of the bottom floor to make sure it was chud free then made our way to the second floor via the stairwell. Steve and Craig said the queens lived on the second floor, so we went to check on them first. They took us to apartment 2-D and, when we got there, saw that the front door was slightly ajar. Hilary nudged it open with the business end of her shotgun and saw no one inside. At the back of the apartment a window was open. Steve called out to the queens but got no response. Hilary had us wait in the hall and took Sanchez into the apartment with her. They went room to room, finding no one, then went to the open window to close it.

"Steve! Craig! I think I found your friends." We entered the apartment and joined her at the window. As we got closer, we could see it was not open but broken through. I leaned out the window to take a look and saw two very dead people on the pavement below, surrounded by broken glass. One of the queens had his throat ripped out; the other queen was the chud that did it. As near as I could piece together, one had turned chud and attacked the other one, then they both went out the window. The

33

chud/queen had to have landed on its head and broken its neck, which is why it wasn't still chewing on the other. Neither Steve nor Craig wanted to look, but Steve finally did just to confirm their identities.

"Yeah, it's them," he confirmed to Hilary. Then he turned to Craig, "Looks like we ain't getting paid." We left the apartment through the front door and closed it behind us.

"Jill, which apartment does your online friend live in?" Hilary asked.

"I'm not exactly sure, I just know he lives in this building," Jill replied. "I can try to get him through Instant Messenger and see if he's here." She pulled out her cell phone and loaded the Instant Messenger app.

"It says here he's online; let me send him a message." Jill typed something into the phone and hit send. There was almost an immediate response.

"He's alive! He says he's in 4-B, to come on up." Jill put away her phone and started to make her way to the stairs, with Katie right behind her. Hilary stopped them before they could make any progress to the next floor.

"We have to check out the third floor first," she hissed, "we can't just go running up there." Jill looked disappointed, but nodded in acknowledgement. We ascended to the third floor and saw that all of the apartments were closed and there were no chuds in the hallway. Hilary signaled for us to follow her up the stairs to the fourth floor. Jill looked like she could barely contain herself. Hilary nudged the fourth floor stairwell door open and peered down the hallway. Apartment 4-B was to our right at the northeast end of the hallway, but between us and that door were two chuds facing away from us. Hilary signaled to Chip Younger to flank her.

"I'm going to take the one nearest us with the machete. I need you to get the other one with that compound bow of yours. Look, the door to 4-C is standing open; we have to be quiet about this in case there's more inside." Hilary crept toward the closest chud and Younger took aim at the second one. Using all of her strength, Hilary swung the machete at the chud, and managed to bury it in the wall: the hallway wasn't wide enough for her to take such a large swing. Younger let fly with his arrow, nailing his target square in the base of the skull, felling it instantly. He notched another arrow and took aim at the chud Hilary was supposed to take out; she was busy trying to remove her machete from the wall. The chud, hearing the commotion, turned around to face Hilary.

"Shit, I've got no shot!" Younger cursed. Before anyone could respond, Stan Gunkle ran forward and cleaved the chuds head in half with a fire axe then booted it down the hallway with a vicious front thrust kick that caught the chud square in the chest. He spun around to Hilary and asked her if she was okay.

"Yeah, thanks, Pops...forgot about the width of the hallway." Hilary looked ashamed, as if she was embarrassed that she had to be saved yet again, this time by an old man.

"No trouble, sweetheart, just looking out for you like I would anyone else in our little family here." Stan looked at her in a grandfatherly manner and squeezed her shoulder. "Now let's try to get that blade out of the wall." The two of them together extracted the machete from the wall, all the while keeping an eye on the open door of apartment 4-C. They rejoined the group, and we decided that Stan, Hilary, Chip and I would go investigate 4-C to make sure it was clear. Stan gave Edith a peck on the cheek and told her he would be right back. She smiled at him, stroked his face and said nothing. The four of us made our way to the open door with Chip and Stan at both sides, Hilary directly in front and me to her left. The door was only open about halfway, so Hilary squatted down and nudged it all the way open with her blade. All the apartments had the same floor plan and square footage. How they were decorated and furnished varied wildly from one tenant to the next. The queen's apartment, for example, had been light and airy. Furnished with taste and tact. The resident of 4-C, on the other hand, could have very easily been one of those people who played Dungeons and Dragons for a good part of his youth, and may still to this day. The sparse entryway opened to the living room that contained a brown sectional couch which faced a huge television with speakers positioned all around it. There were posters on the walls advertising various Japanese anime movies like "Ninja Scroll", "Vampire Hunter 'D'" and "Akira". Numerous video game consoles were all attached to a central hub, which in turn was attached to the massive television. There was a coffee table positioned between the couch and TV. On it were several video game magazines, two remote controls and an enormous glass bong which was very dirty from extensive use. We walked past the living room, saw the dining area was empty and went down the hall to the bedroom/bathroom area. We entered the bedroom and saw that it, too, was empty, but that the bathroom door was closed. There was a noise from behind the closed door. It sounded like a muffled cough. Hilary signaled for Chip and Stan to flank the door. She walked up to it and put her ear against it. Another muffled cough. Hilary backed up and pointed at her foot then at the door. We all understood she meant to kick it in and to be on the ready for whatever was behind the door. She held up her hand and counted to three on her fingers then kicked in the bathroom door. Sitting on the toilet was a little Asian guy, maybe Vietnamese, smoking a pipe and coughing into a towel. The smell of marijuana billowed into the room with a cloud of smoke like a bank of fog. The little man gave out a shriek.

"Ahhhhhh!" he said. "AAhhhh...AAAAHHH!" He held the pipe out in front of him, brandishing it like a weapon, then he realized we weren't chuds and lowered his hands. Then, seeing our weapons and the amount of blood on some of us, raised them again.

"Look, if you're here to rob me, I don't have much, you can probably get something for the Xbox and Playstation, but I don't have much cash on hand...here, take my weed , you can probably sell that for more!" He held out a baggie that had a generous amount of green in it. I surmised that it was most likely "good shit" from the lingering aroma in the air. I noticed Chip raise an eyebrow at the sight of the baggie.

"No, we're not here to rob you," Hilary said. "We were just checking to make sure there were no more of those things on this floor. We're actually on our way to your neighbors; one of our group is friendly with him. I'm Hilary, and you are?"

"Victor Nguyen. I saw the shit going down on TV and then I heard some commotion in the hallway. That's when I locked myself in here. I don't remember what time that was."

"We came in here because your door was open and there were two nasties in the hallway. We had to make sure there were none in here. Do you know anything about your neighbor?"

"I game with him sometimes, but I hardly ever see him outside of his apartment. He's a real introvert. I don't even think I know his real name, just his gamer name."

"Well, you're welcome to come with us, if you like, or you can stay here. Your choice."

"Where are you guys going? How many of you are there?" Nguyen asked.

"We plan on getting to the top floor of this building and fortify there. We're just trying to round up survivors and clear the building of any more of those things. Once we establish a base of operations, so to speak, we can figure out what to do and where to go from there. My number one concern is getting us safe and secure. Right now there are fifteen—no wait, fourteen of us. We lost the lawyer before we got in here."

"Well, I suppose safety in numbers," Nguyen replied. "I'm with you guys."

"You got any weapons or supplies you can pack up?" Hilary asked.

"I got some food and stuff, but the closest I have to a weapon would be Casper the Friendly Toke out there. That's the name of my bong," he said proudly with a wide smile.

"Well, grab the food and whatever else you might think will be helpful and let's get out of here," Hilary said. "We still have to visit next door and clear one more floor before we can get to my people and see if they're still with us."

"You can't call them?" I asked Hilary. "It would seem that the phones and electricity are still working."

"They aren't phone kind of people. We usually communicate through other means."

"Mmmm-kay," I said. "Very mysterious, but whatever. Let's just get to the top and figure this all out." Nguyen had returned with a backpack loaded with junk food and Ramen noodles.

"Let's boogie," he said, "I feel safer already." We left Nguyen's apartment and went back to the group that were still hanging out in the stairwell between the third and fourth floors. Edith Gunkle got weepy at the sight of Stan returning as she ran forward and grabbed him in a bear hug.

"Oh, Stan, I was so worried!" she said, looking into his eyes.

"Have faith in the old man, dumpling! I can hold my own with these young-uns!" he replied with a grin and a twinkle in his eye. Victor Nguyen was introduced to the group, after which Hilary turned to Jill.

"Okay, time to go meet your boyfriend...you at least know his name, right?"

"Yes! And he's not my boyfriend! His name is Mike Hunt." We all burst out laughing. Jill apparently didn't get the joke.

"What? What's so funny?"

"You really don't get it?" I asked.

"Get what? I don't understand."

"Think about how it's pronounced. Mike Hunt. Run it together a little quicker and what does it sound like?" I could see Jill thinking it over in her head and then she started to voice it.

"Mike Hunt, mikehunt, mikehunt, mykunt, my cunt...OH, GODDAMMITT!" We all started laughing again.

"I'm sure he's a charming fellow," Hilary said, stifling her giggles, "but fact is, someone's in that apartment and we need to add to the ranks and clear this floor. So Jill, if you will please, take us to Mr. Hunt." The sincerity with which Hilary delivered this last line sent us all in to hysterics. Jill had turned a deep shade of crimson, but pushed her way to the front of the group and started to make her way to apartment 4B. She strode up to the door and knocked rapidly. We could hear someone thudding up to the door, then the sound of locks disengaging. The door opened but Jill was the only person with a vantage point to actually see the occupant. We saw her face break in to a wide grin and then we heard a voice issue forth from the open doorway.

"Michael Oliver Hunt, at your service." Jill looked over at us with a raised eyebrow. We looked at each other with shrugged shoulders. The occupant came through the doorway and we all got a good look at him, and he was gorgeous. And I'm not even remotely attracted to men. But this guy might as well have had a sunbeam following him wherever he went. He was about 6'3", chiseled features, bronze skin, curly black hair, piercing blue eyes and a smile that seemed to have a glint to it when it caught the light just so. He turned his gaze from Jill to us, and I could have sworn that there was a mass swooning from the feminine members of the group. Jeff Clark seemed unimpressed.

"Please, everyone, come in," Mike Hunt invited. "There's room enough for all of you, but seating may be limited." He retreated to his apartment and Jill followed. The rest of us slowly made our way, with Steve and Craig bringing up the rear and closing the door behind us. It seemed that Mr. Hunt was quite the techie. The living room of his apartment featured a solid wall of computer monitors with a table in front of it that contained two laptop computers with a mouse pad and wireless mouse between them. I noticed all the windows were covered up and completely blacked out. Mike Hunt sat on a corner of the table and addressed us.

"Yes, Mike Hunt is my real name. Let's just get that out of the way. Now, it's good to see so many survivors in one group. Including you, Victor. You were wise enough to go to high ground, I assume you're a smart bunch, or at least some of you are anyway. Does anybody know what's happening here?"

"All I know is, I woke up this morning with my little sister being chewed on by my father and I took action," Hilary said. She waved a hand at the wall of computer screens. "What's all this?"

"This," Mike said, making a hand gesture of his own toward the wall of screens, "is what's happening here." We all looked more intently at the computer screens. Most were news reports from various stations located around the country. Based on the information printed at the bottom of each screen, we could see all the reporters were broadcasting from the same area: just outside of our town. We also noticed that each and every one of those reporters was standing in front of a chain link fence.

"Bring up the sound on that one," Hilary said, pointing at a screen in the middle that was showing a national newscast. Mike turned to one of the laptops and made it happen.

"...and quickly erected the fence you see behind me, effectively sealing in the town. We have a graphic we're going to show in a moment that will demonstrate where the accident happened and the radius of the cloud. Before we do that, though, to recap: at 12:40 a.m. a tanker truck in a military convoy blew a tire and overturned on Interstate 95 that runs through the north side of the town. The overturned truck was carrying a highly dangerous experimental biological weapon that was en route to disposal, whose contents were released when the accident occurred. From what information the military has divulged over the last few hours, the weapon was gaseous in nature, and that initial cloud is what has been confirmed to have caused the outbreak. The weapon was designed to attack people of a certain blood type when it was airborne, then those affected peoples would transmit the effect through blood transmission, either through biting or scratching. Although the cloud itself dissipated after about fifteen minutes, you'll see in the graphic the affected area. Some of the men in the military convoy were affected, turning on their comrades and spurning the initial spread of the condition. Since the cloud has dissipated, it is theorized that there are no chances of the condition occurring through airborne means, only through contact with one of the infected. As such, the military has quarantined the entire town and have set up the fence behind me. They were able to erect the main fence line very quickly, establish the first barrier and have now constructed four additional layers with only two entry/exit points. No one is being allowed to exit the town, however, I'm told by the commanding officer on scene that all residents are restricted from exiting for at least the foreseeable future. Only military personnel are allowed to enter, but at this point, none have been instructed to do so." Hilary told Mike to kill the sound; she looked towards her feet and started biting her bottom lip. She looked up at the wall of screens and scanned each one. Then she pointed at one towards the top right.

"There," she said, "that one is positioned just west of here. Let's lock this building down, and then we can send a small group to that area and see if we can negotiate our way out of this. They say they aren't letting anyone out; we need to see if we can change their minds about that. We have one more floor to clear. My people are on that floor as well, so two birds, one stone." She instructed everybody to stay put and chose myself, Chip and Stan to go with her upstairs. Most everybody seemed pleased with this and started to get settled. Mike and Jill had broken off from the group and were having a quiet conversation. We exited Mike's place and went back to the stairwell. We went up to the fifth floor and saw nothing unusual in the hallway. I asked Hilary which apartment we needed to go to. She said 5-A was our ultimate destination, but that we had to clear the other apartments first. Apartments 5-B and 5-C were both unlocked and empty. Apartment 5-D was unlocked, but not empty. There was a body on the floor right behind the door, its face gone; I surmised it had been chewed off. We silently entered the apartment and heard noises from the back bedroom. With Hilary in the lead we crept down the hallway. When we got to the door she silently turned the knob and nudged it open. It opened noiselessly and we peered into the room. It was a chud, of course, just bumbling around the room. Since they hadn't learned how to operate doorknobs yet, it most likely had gotten stuck in there after chewing his friend's face off. It hadn't detected us yet, so Hilary signaled to Chip to get in position and make ready. Chip backed up and raised the bow and took aim. He nodded to Hilary and she nodded back; he released the arrow. The chud dropped instantly. We silently congratulated Chip and turned to leave. We returned to the front room and regarded the body on the floor. Chip stuck an arrow in the base of its skull, just to be on the safe side.

"Okay, we have to be prepared for the eventuality that your friends may be in the same condition," Stan said to Hilary.

"Yeah, I'm aware of that, Pops. Let's just get this over with." We made our way to 5-A and Hilary didn't try the door. She just knocked softly three times, then two, followed by a single knock.

"What is this, your secret clubhouse?" I snickered. She punched me in the shoulder, hard.

"Shhh, fool!" From the other side of the door came a voice, very male and very gruff.

"Yeah, who is it?"

"It's Hilary Beasley." There was the sound of a lock disengaging and the door cracked open. A big, black dude peered out at us. I immediately thought of Michael Clarke Duncan as John Coffey in the film version of Stephen King's "The Green Mile". The black dude looked at the three of us that weren't Hilary Beasley and he appeared unimpressed.

"The fuck you want?" The three of us that weren't Hilary Beasley took a step back. Hilary was unfazed and pushed right past the man-mountain into the apartment. The rest of us didn't move. He looked back at her, then to us and motioned for us to enter. We stepped through the doorway, "Try a Little Tenderness" by Otis Redding was playing softly somewhere in the room.

"Don't act so tough, Sharp, these guys are friends," Hilary said. "There are some more downstairs, in 4-B."

"How many?"

"Twelve more, besides us."

"Any of them yo' family?" Hilary shook her head and looked at the floor.

"None of them made it. Ortega over there was the first living person I came across."

"Danny Ortega," I said, extending a hand to Sharp. He took it and gave it a pump. My hand disappeared inside of his.

"Just call me Sharp," he said and turned his attention back to Hilary. "Sorry to hear 'bout yo' family. Yo' ol' man was a good dude, good businessman. An' he was a good dad to you an' Rachel, sorry 'bout her, too. What's yo' plan?"

"Right now, lock the building down. We've secured all the apartments that weren't locked and have dispatched a couple of those things in the hallways. If there's any more in the building, they're behind locked doors. Where's the other two?"

"They in the back, doing inventory."

"Okay, I'll bring them up to speed in a minute. I saw a news report that says they've sealed in the town. I want to take a group to the west entrance to see if I can talk to somebody in charge and get us out of here."

"Yeah, we seen that, too. Me and the boys figured we'd just lock down and chill. Give it a day or two. Make a move afer that. You an yo' homies poppin' up changes that some." Sharp sat on the arm of the couch and crossed his arms over his broad chest.

"We could use you and the twins for manpower, and your arsenal for firepower. Without you we could probably survive this. With you we can all definitely survive this. If I can't talk our way out of here at that entry point, we have to be ready to ride this thing out. If they don't let us out of here, the only other option we have is to wipe every single last one of those undead mother fuckers from this town. So the only question I have is, are you with us or are you dead men?" Sharp's mouth lifted into a half-smile, and he chuckled deeply.

"Yo' old man said you was a bad bitch, and now I done seen it fo' myself. A'ight, Beasley. We got yo' back. Twins and me, this our block. Ain't no zombie-ass mutha fuckas takin' our shit." Hilary stuck her hand out to Sharp, but he just enveloped her in a big bear hug then let her go. "A'ight, Boss, what we doin'?"

"Let me go talk to the Dayze Boyz, then we can regroup with the rest and figure out who's making the journey to that gate. Ortega, come with me for a sec." She started to make her way to the back of the apartment towards the master bedroom area. We had gotten about halfway down the hall when she stopped and turned to me, so abruptly that I ran right in to her with enough force that I instinctively reached out to grab her to prevent her from toppling over. In doing so, I noticed that she was trembling all over, so I did what my next instincts told me to do and drew her near and brought her in my embrace. She allowed it, and since we were the same height, instead of laying her head on my chest and sobbing, she did it on my shoulder. I could feel the hot tears seeping into my shirt sleeve, but I didn't mind. I didn't say anything, either; I didn't want to interrupt whatever it was she was letting out. She didn't say anything at first. The crying lasted about ninety seconds then she stopped almost as suddenly as she started, raised her head and looked into my eyes with her red and teary ones. She gave me a passionate kiss on the lips that lasted for about ten seconds in real time, but in my time, from first mouth contact to final lip disengage, it was about a century. My eyes were open the entire time, just staring at her lovely, slightly blood-encrusted face as she nonverbally thanked me for being there right when she needed somebody. She pulled back, opened her eyes and looked into mine again, verbalizing it.

"Thank you, Danny, for being there. Now, then, whatever is coming...I already feel like I can depend on you. And you're easy on the eyes, so bonus there. I know you're not big on the fighting thing, but I think we make a great team regardless."

"Well, despite the mini-apocalypse going on outside and the fact that we both lost our families today, that is one of the best things that has ever happened to me." She punched me in the shoulder again, but not quite as hard and a smile was cracking her lips.

"Fool," she said, shaking her head. "Come on, let's go talk to the twins and work on our next move. Thanks for letting me get emotional for a second there." She gave me another kiss and turned to walk down the hallway.

"So does this mean we're dating or...," I said to the back of her head. She didn't respond, so I just followed her to the back room where her other two friends were . The door was closed but Hilary didn't bother to knock on this one, she opened it and went right in. Inside the room there was no bedroom furniture, just stacks of wooden crates. There were also two identical looking men in the room. One was opening wooden crates and the other was holding a clipboard, writing down whatever the other guy was telling him. They were both light-skinned black men, with light brown, close-cropped afros that were about three inches in length. Upon entering the room, both men looked in our direction and I could see that they were indeed twins; it wasn't just a moniker.

"Danny Ortega, meet Joshua and Jacob Dayze." Neither one of them was nearly as threatening as Sharp had been, quite the contrary, they were both quite friendly. They introduced themselves to me individually and told me the best way to tell them apart was that Joshua always had a pair of aviator sunglasses on his person. Today, for instance, they were hanging from the front of his shirt neckline. We made small talk for a couple of minutes then I asked what was in the crates.

"Guns," Jacob and Joshua said simultaneously. I looked at Hilary, then around the room; there were a LOT of crates. I guess Hilary could sense I was going to start bubbling up with questions, so she just started to explain.

"My dad and Sharp were in business together as arms dealers. My dad wanted me to take over his business for him, but I was a little reluctant. I've been involved in this since a young age, but it's never what I wanted to do. Still, my old man would take me out to the range to practice shooting or bring me on deals. After a while I just kind of accepted my role in things and got adapted to the lifestyle."

"Well, that would explain why your family has...had a rough reputation in this town. Who do you sell to, terrorists?" I inquired.

"No, nothing like that. The people we get the guns from aren't the first link in the chain nor are the people we give them to the last. Where they eventually wind up is anybody's guess, we just facilitate them getting there. It's not glamorous or legal, but it's also not drugs and it keeps the bills paid."

"In this instance, you're the exact person I'd want to be around, glamorous or not."

Hilary turned her attention back to the Dayze twins and let them know her plan to put a group together to go to the gate. She told them she wanted them to stick around here and watch over the rest of the group while she, Sharp, Chip, Dirty Sanchez and myself would make the journey. I was about to protest, but she put a finger to my lips and stifled me. She explained that she wanted me as a spotter, that the rest of the manpower would have enough weapons to take care of any threats. I was okay with that and told her so. We went back to the guys in the living room where Hilary laid out her plan. Everyone signed on for the plan and we gathered some weapons to take with us back down to 4-B.

We rejoined the rest of the group in Mike Hunt's apartment and filled everyone else in on the goings-on. Everybody seemed on board with the exception of Jethro and the McMullens, who were passed out on the floor. We decided we would get some rest and leave at first light. It was already starting to get dark outside and we didn't want to take our chances with these things with little to no light. Mike Hunt suggested that some of us retreat to other unoccupied apartments so we weren't all crammed in one space. We were relatively sure that the building was safe; at least the open apartments were, anyway. A few of us meandered off to get some shuteye. Victor said a few people could come with him to his apartment, and Hilary and I went with Sharp and the Dayze twins back to their apartment. Hilary and I slept together that night, but not in a sexual way; neither of us was feeling particularly sexy. We just lay together and held each other and drifted off to dream-land, a land that was thankfully not full of chuds.

The next morning, the five of us taking the trip stocked up on necessary items: weapons and ammo for them, binoculars for me. I felt like the world's most guarded bird-watcher. We said our goodbyes to the group and they gave us their "good lucks". We descended back to the first floor and exited the building. I took a good look around. I saw plenty of dead people but none of them were reanimated. Everywhere I looked there was no movement, except for things that stirred in the light breeze. We started to make our way west, towards where the gate would be. About two blocks from the apartments the buildings were rarely over a story tall. We could see the sky over where the gate would be located. It was filled with news choppers and military vehicles. Every once in a while, one of them would fly over the town; I don't know if they saw us or not. We continued to make our way to the gate. I hadn't seen any chuds and I told the group that it worried me.

"Why do you call them 'chuds', Ortega?" Sharp asked.

"There was this old 1980's horror movie called 'C.H.U.D.', it stood for 'Cannibalistic Humanoid Underground Dwellers'. Anyway, that's what popped in my head when I saw these things. I know they're not underground dwellers, per se, but that's just semantics. And I think the word 'zombie' is way over-played."

"Fair enough."

We walked a couple of blocks and then I saw a motion out of the corner of my eye. I halted the group and we looked in the direction where I had seen movement. Sure enough, it was a chud shambling westward. Although shambling wasn't exactly correct. That's how they moved earlier; this one seemed to be loping, almost like a light jog. We dropped in noiselessly behind it, about twenty yards back. I checked to make sure there were no more behind us and we started to follow the chud. We walked a few more blocks and I halted the group again. To our left were three chuds, also going westward. It was starting to appear that we all had the same destination in mind. We rounded a bend in the road and could see the fence. There were chuds swarming all around it. The only thing we could figure was that they were drawn here by all the action and commotion caused by the military and news teams. There were a few abandoned cars and a Greyhound bus on the road before the gate and fence. Hilary said we should make our way to the bus and climb on top of it, and then we should be able to get the attention of whoever was on the other side of the fence. We had a direct line to the back of the bus and, with Sharp in the group, we wouldn't have any trouble climbing it. We got to the bus uneventfully and climbed to the top. Once there, we could see the other people on the outside of the fence. We started to shout and wave our arms to get their attention. Within a few seconds, one of the military personnel spotted us and called out to another soldier. They acknowledged us and waved back; one of the soldiers had a megaphone and addressed us.

"Survivors! Stay where you are and our commanding officer will talk to you shortly." Some of the chuds had become aware of our presence and were starting to surround the bus. After about two minutes of waiting, the commanding officer of the unit appeared on the scene and spoke to us through the megaphone.

"Hello, it's good to see some people are still alive in there. If any of you has a cell phone on you, please call this number and we can discuss the situation. 555-1219." Dirty Sanchez said that he still had his phone on him, and luckily it still had three-quarters of a battery charge. Hilary dialed the number and put the phone on speaker, so we could all hear what the officer had to say. The phone was answered after two rings.

"Hello, this is Major Tom Willis, United States Army. Who am I speaking with?"

"This is Hilary Beasley, townsperson. I'm here with part of my group; we have fifteen other survivors at the King's Arms Apartments. I don't know if there are other survivors besides us, I just speak for our group. What is the possibility of getting us out of here and to safety?"

"I'm afraid we can't allow anyone in or out for the foreseeable future. We can't take the chance of any infected getting out, so for now the gates must remain closed. My suggestion is to fortify yourselves and try to wait this thing out. We're still trying to figure out what to do about these things, there's a lot we don't know. Until we figure out how to stop them or wipe them all out, the gate stays closed." Hilary stayed silent for a moment; clearly this wasn't what she wanted to hear.

"What if we helped to exterminate them from the inside? If we can reduce their numbers or wipe them out completely, could we be let out then?"

"Theoretically, yes, if there aren't any more of those things to pose a threat and it's clear that none of your group are infected. This may take some time, though; I hope you're ready for the long haul."

"I think we have enough weapons and ammo to take care of the problem," Hilary said, "and I think we should start right here." To emphasize her point, she withdrew her revolver and plugged a chud in the head that was bumbling around the bus. The major came back over the phone.

"I can't officially ask you to do this, but if this is the course of action you wish to take, I can't stop you either. Frankly it's the best idea we have right now, short of dropping a bomb on the town." I couldn't tell if he was joking or not. Hilary hung up the phone after signing off with the major then surveyed the chuds surrounding the bus.

"Let's go back the way we came. We have to clear some of these shits out first. Concentrate on the ones towards the rear of the bus and we'll cut a path out of here." I was only armed with binoculars, so I couldn't clear anything, but the rest of the guys did just fine without me. After felling enough to give us a clear way off the bus and back to the apartments, we climbed down and got the hell out of there. On the way back, we encountered a few chuds here and there; we took them all out. We made it back to the King's Arms and went to break the news to the rest of the group. Most understood and reluctantly accepted what we had to face and what we'd have to do to get out of here. The only holdouts were Jethro and the McMullens who only wanted to get out of here to chase their next high. We were able to bring them around eventually, but also knew they weren't going to be much help. We chose the sentries that would be positioned on the rooftop to be spotters and snipers, and then selected the group of people that would be going out to do battle. Dirty Sanchez, Mike Hunt and the Dayze twins would serve as sentries; Hilary, Chip, Stan, Sharp and I would be the hunting group. The rest of our group of survivors would serve as the support team: cooking, cleaning, first aid, whatever. We decided to go out every other day: rest one day and hunt the next. I was reluctant to accept my role at first, but if it meant spending more time with Hilary, so be it. I knew that she'd have my back and protect me, as well as I'd have hers and protect her the best I could.

We know what day it is outside of the Q-Zone, or Quarantine Zone, but inside, to us, its 200 A.Z., two hundred days since the outbreak. We survivors are going to wipe out the rest of those chuds and get that fence to come down. We've been making good progress, even have a couple of vehicles outfitted to help with our hunts and give us more protection while we're out there. As for right now, we're getting a little crew together to make a Wal-Mart run. It seems we need to get more toilet paper, ammo and canned goods. Also, Hilary and I need to get a pregnancy test.

Another Day at the Office

"Sometimes, it's just like…ugh…I just don't have it in me anymore."

 Hurng and Korgath were sidling down the dimly lit corridor with its pockmarked walls, Hurng looking more dejected than usual. They turned the corner and started down the steps that led to the doorway that led to their ready-room. Korgath gave Hurng a sideways glance.

"You've got some parasites on you. Right there, on your neck bone." Hurng flicked them off with a lazy swish of his tail and they splatted against the wall. "It's Shielka again, isn't it?"

"Well, yes and no," Hurng said. "Yes, she brought it up, but I've been feeling like this for a while."

"Come on, it's like I told you before. You're a demon, it's not like you can take ballet lessons and join Cirque du Soleil."

"I know, I know," Hurng muttered. "I just feel like I'm meant for more than menial grunt work. I want to move up the chain a little bit, maybe get a better cave with a nice outcropping..."

"OK, now that's definitely Shielka talking. At least you're staying in your own ballpark this time with this 'moving up the chain' business."

Korgath stopped and turned to his partner, grasping him by his shoulders with his upper two arms and by the wrists with his lower two. "It's not going to come easy to you. You have to use your own two arms and work for it." He shook Hurng gently as punctuation. They were outside the door to their ready-room; Korgath turned to it and spoke the words to gain entry.

"Hemhash forash, de bominus, le locus leiis!" The stone door slid open and the two demons entered the room.

"You remember Scrax, yeah? That guy went up two levels when he pulled The Krakauer Job. Use something like that for inspiration." Korgath was trying his very best to cheer up his partner because he didn't want to have to deal with this mood all day. It seemed to work a little bit.

"Yeah," Hurng said, smiling a little "The Krakauer Job! I could do something like that!"

"Sure, and just put the ol' Hurng spin on it! Look, buddy, you're one of the best soul stealers in this sector, and I'm not just saying that to twist your horns."

"I think I can do better than The Krakauer Job, much better. Scrax pulled, what, four at once? I'm gonna do six and not at The Krakauer Convalescence Home. I'm going to the Needham State Penitentiary; I'm going after some real bad-asses. Thanks, Korgath! I don't know why I didn't think of this before. Hey, why don't you come with me? We can make it a dozen and both move up a few levels!"

"Whoa, buddy, not this guy. I'm perfectly content where I'm at. I have no dreams and aspirations of moving up any levels, of getting drafted to the army, or getting thrust into any service other than the collecting I already do. I'll do my ten hours, take a succubus back to my cave every once in a while. Hell, I even have this pint of infant blood I'm saving for a special occasion. They don't let you have infant blood when you start moving up levels and such. They say it's too intoxicating; they need sharp minds on the upper levels and in the army. Did you know that in the army, sometimes they take you and squeeze you into a human body to be a spy on the living world and see what the other half is up to? That happened to a cousin of mine, he was never the same after that. Kept babbling about a television show, said he needed to find out what happened next to Scooby and the gang. Nope, perfectly content." Korgath leaned back against the wall and took a deep breath, his three nostrils flaring.

"Hey, pal, if it works for you, then so be it. I know I'm destined for greatness and, thanks to your advice, I know how I'm going to achieve it." Hurng turned and grabbed the black globe from the center of the pedestal that was his work station. He held it out in front of him with both hands and stared intently into it. He closed his eyes and, with an audible pop, Hurng and the black globe disappeared, shifting through time and space on their way to Needham State Penitentiary. Korgath sighed and walked over to his own pedestal and looked at the black globe positioned there. On the wall above the pedestal was a list of souls for the day and where to find them. Korgath shifted his gaze from the globe to the list. Just then, the door slid open behind him and someone entered the room. Korgath looked at the new occupant. She was gorgeous! Slick, purple skin covered a sinewy frame that bulged at the hips. Coarse, black hair spilled all the way down her back while yellow eyes stared at him from underneath a furrowed brow. Her fat, pink lips began to move as she spoke to him.

"H-hi, I'm Q'erthy. I'm new here." She thrust a fistful of paperwork at Korgath. He took it from her and smoothed it out with his four hands to get a good look at it.

"Let's see: 'Blah-blah-blah, Q'erthy Pung, blah-blah-blah, new partner, more blah...oh, Hurng ordered this, good man! Seems he's moved up already!" Korgath folded the papers and handed them back to Q'erthy . "Well, welcome then. I was expecting a new partner, but this is a pleasant surprise." There was another audible pop in the room and a black globe replaced the empty spot on the pedestal that had once been Hurng's. Korgath motioned towards the soul list above his pedestal.

"Well there's the list, you should know about that already. Now, you won't be going alone for your first couple of days. We'll go as a team until you get the hang of things...what was your score on the TF Test?"

"Perfect 100%," Q'erthy said proudly. Korgath was impressed. Hurng had sent him a really good one.

"OK, right then. You may just need a few trips before going solo." Q'erthy had walked up to the list; Korgath was behind her and couldn't take his eye off of those hips. She spun around suddenly, three breasts jiggling, with her hands clasped together.

"Can we get started?" she asked excitedly. "I've been dying to get a real one. Those practice souls really don't put up a fight. Right before graduation I was grabbing six or seven at a time. Some of the more jealous kids called me a showoff." Korgath smiled at her and patted her on her shoulder.

"Sure, kid. Let's get started." Korgath pointed at the first name on the list. "Perkins. Ryan. Age 32. Location: New York City. Year: 2016. Alright, let's do it." Korgath motioned to Q'erthy's globe. She picked it up and held it in front of her. Korgath picked up his own globe and held it with two of his four hands.

"Now, I'm going to take the lead on this one, so you just focus on the name and location. I'll take care of the travel arrangements." Q'erthy nodded silently and started to bite her bottom lip nervously. They both stared into their globes then closed their eyes. Korgath spoke to the room. There was a flash and then dark. They both peered around in the darkness, getting familiar with their surroundings. Korgath took a step forward and bumped into a couch, where a sleeping man snorted and farted. Korgath looked at him, but it wasn't their quarry. Perkins would be found in a back room down the hallway. The sleeping man on the couch rolled over and snored heavily, an empty bottle of Jack Daniel's on the floor near his head. He had a pair of headphones on connected to an iPod. It was turned up loud enough you could hear Megadeth's

"Symphony of Destruction" pouring out. Korgath pointed down the hall to the room where their target lay. Q'erthy nodded and fell in behind Korgath, moving down the hall silently. They came to a closed door and Korgath opened it slowly, peering inside the new room. There was a bed inside with a figure on it, apparently asleep. They entered the room and took up positions opposite each other on either side of the bed. Up to this point, it seemed fairly routine and Korgath had no reason to think otherwise. He and the rookie would now take this guy's soul, return to their dimension and move on to the next name on the list. Repeat process. That's what they did. The souls would be stored in their globes and at the end of the day they were harvested and sent to "The Factory" where they were turned into something else. Korgath didn't know much more than that, he was just a collector. He really didn't need to know much. Back in this guy's dimension, the guy on the couch would wake up and find this guy dead from natural causes, because your heart kind of stops when the soul is removed from it.

Korgath looked over the bed at Q'erthy, she was even more beautiful in this dull moonlight, and the shadows accentuated all her curves just the right way. He licked his lips and decided that after their shift he would ask her back to his cave for some infant blood and see if they could become partners outside of the office.

"You wanna take this one?" he whispered at her quietly.

"Can I?" she asked gleefully. Korgath nodded and she smiled widely. She jumped up and down a couple of times and Korgath found himself almost hypnotized by those three perfect bouncing breasts. She held her globe out in front of her; you could tell she was concentrating very hard. It didn't matter how good you were with the practice souls, human souls were a little tricky to get the hang of at the start. Korgath remembered his first soul and how the bastard had kept trying to squirt away. He remembered Hurng's first soul, when Hurng had tripped over a bassinet in this log cabin and gone ass-over-tea kettle. He'd held on to that soul the whole time, but boy was the expression on his face as he went backwards over that bassinet priceless. Now here was this rookie, Q'erthy, pulling her first soul, and looking damn fine trying to do it. Her globe gave off a dull light even though it remained pitch black in color. The body on the bed began to give off a different light, a brighter one that was indicative of the soul coming out. But then the light did a queer thing, something Korgath had neither ever seen nor heard of before. The light coming out of the body took on a shape and from Korgath's perspective, that shape was a closed fist. Korgath tilted his head to the side like a puppy and looked at the shape, dumbfounded. Q'erthy apparently didn't see this; she was too busy concentrating on her globe. Korgath watched as the light fist formed and then reared back. Before he could say anything it plunged forward towards Q'erthy and her globe. Korgath stared, unblinking as she exploded into a purple/green mist and her globe shattered and turned to dust as the light fist struck her. Korgath stood there, statuesque as the remains of Q'erthy dripped off of the ceiling and walls, and himself. The light fist turned towards Korgath and did another queer thing: it turned sideways and flipped him the finger before retreating back into the body from whence it came. Korgath came back to his senses in a rush and shook his head to clear the cobwebs. The light fist was gone, the body still slept soundlessly in its bed, and Q'erthy was still vaporized. Korgath scrambled back towards the door of the room and then looked at his globe, willing himself back to the office. With a flash and a pop, he was back in front of his pedestal where he placed his globe, then started shaking all over. What in the blue hell had just happened? Before he could contemplate more, the door to his office slid open and there stood Hurng. He strode in and walked up to Korgath, looking his former partner in the eye as he did.

"What just happened up there?"

Korgath related the details as best he could to Hurng, from the sleeping, farting man, to the light fist, to Q'erthy dripping off the walls and holy shit there was still some on him. Hurng tried to calm his former partner down, said that he would take the information upstairs. He patted Korgath on one of his shoulders and told him he had done a good thing. Korgath looked at Hurng, agog. Hurng explained that they may have just found a soul they had been looking for, one they had been in search of for well over millennia now. Korgath grasped the brevity of the statement right away. If they had been looking for this soul for millennia down here, that translated into a hell of a lot longer up there. Hurng told his former partner to take the rest of the day off, maybe go drink that infant blood. Korgath agreed, said he planned on doing the whole bottle. Hurng chuckled, patted his friend on the back and walked him out. Korgath made his way out of the place he worked and turned toward his cave, head slumped. He suddenly felt so tired.

Hurng gave his friend one last wave as he disappeared over the horizon then went back inside. He had important information to take upstairs and, after his recent promotion (after what was already being referred to as "The Needham Incident" around the office), this would be icing on the cake.

See, he was bucking to be one of those demons they squished down and crammed inside of a human body. He was so desperate to be a spy. The levels he'd moved up after Needham were good, but he wanted a taste of the other side. Of course, he'd never told Korgath this. He'd always just expressed his ambition. The information he had now would be exactly what he needed to join the spy ranks. The lift taking him to the executive floor couldn't move fast enough.

Hurng practically leapt off the lift when it got to the executive floor. He approached The Boss's secretary and announced his presence and intentions. She told him to wait a few minutes and called in to The Boss. After a short conversation she waved him over and opened the door, ushering him inside. Hurng entered eagerly and the door shut behind him. The room was basically empty with the exception of a huge throne of skulls, surrounded by fire, on which sat a sharply dressed man with extremely shiny shoes. The throne was about fifteen feet high, easily triple Hurng's size. The sharply dressed man in the very shiny shoes that sat astride it fit comfortably, even though he was much larger than the throne itself. He had to be thirty feet tall easily. His horned head nearly scraped the ceiling of the barren room. The fire that surrounded the throne gave the room a pleasant, red glow that was also soothingly warm compared to the frigid cold that was the lower floors where the drones worked. On one arm of the throne was a cup holder where the sharply dressed, thirty-foot man had a large goblet filled with what Hurng could smell from across the room: infant's blood. On the other arm of the throne, a hollowed out angel skull had been affixed, filled with writhing, human bodies. The sharply dressed man in the shiny shoes reached into the angel skull and withdrew a handful of the writhing, naked human beings. They were moaning, wailing and crying as he lifted them. He then deposited them in his mouth and crunched upon them with viciously sharp and pointy teeth, silencing them. He washed them down with a swig of infant blood and looked down at Hurng. He wiped his mouth with the back of his hand then picked at his teeth with a bladed finger. He extracted a half-chewed human, flicked it against the wall and it stuck. His voice boomed forth.

"WHAT DO YOU HAVE FOR ME?!?" he said. Hurng dropped to his knees before speaking, out of respect for his boss.

"Sir, Your Excellence and Supreme Being! I have information vital to our cause. One of the drones may have found him!" Hurng beamed while delivering this last statement. The sharply dressed man with the very shiny shoes leaned forward on his throne of skulls, keenly interested.

"HIM?!? WE HAVE FOUND HIM?!? WHERE?!? WHAT HAS TRANSPIRED?!?" Hurng related Korgath's story to The Boss, leaving out none of the details Korgath supplied.

"It has to be him, Your Excellence! It has to be The Big Guy!" Anger flashed in the sharply dressed man's eyes, and Hurng cowered.

"NEVER CAPITALIZE HIS NAME!! I SWORE I ALMOST HEARD ADMIRATION IN YOUR VOICE!!" The fire around the throne increased, as if fueled by the sharply dressed man's anger.

"Never, Sir! You are the Almighty and Exhalted One! He is but a bug. An insect!" Secretly, Hurng WAS impressed. The way Korgath had described that fist and how Q'erthy had exploded in that room was certainly impressive. The sharply dressed man with the extremely shiny shoes had calmed somewhat, the flames around the throne receding. Hurng spoke again to The Boss.

"What do we do now, Sir? What is your plan?" The sharply dressed man stroked his enormous, goateed chin, clearly lost in thought. Finally, his voice boomed across the room.

"I'M GOING TO PASS THIS ALONG TO MANAGEMENT!! I WILL HAVE THEM ENTER A BRAINSTORMING SESSION!! I WILL HAVE THEM COME UP WITH THREE...NO, FOUR WAYS TO PROCEED!! YOU HAVE DONE WELL THIS DAY!! YOUR DESIRE TO BE A SPY SHALL BE

GRANTED!! YOU'LL HAVE YOUR OUTCROPPING, YET!! NOW LEAVE ME!!"

Hurng backed out of The Boss's office, extremely pleased with himself. Sure, they'd lost one of their most promising rookies since, well, himself, but they had found The Big Guy, (whoops, the big guy, can't even capitalize it in your thoughts). He was finally going to get to be a spy and get his outcropping. Maybe that would get that harpy Shielka to finally shut up. He entered the lift and went down to the recruitment floor. He would have to fill out all of his paperwork for a transfer to the spy division and get fitted for a body. He couldn't help but think of Korgath and how that poor sap was comfortable just being a collector. But if it weren't for Korgath, he thought, he wouldn't be here right now. Hurng made a mental note to send Korgath a pint of the best infant's blood he could get his hands on when he got back from spy duty. Hell, it was the least he could do for his old partner.

I Fail, You Fail

Geoff Wexler walked in to his classroom where his current crop of sixth-graders were all fidgeting in their chairs, ready to get this last day of school over with. At the time he had no way of knowing this, but by the end of the day he would be questioning whether or not he wanted to be a teacher anymore, and also if he was going to live to see the next day. He strode towards his desk at the front of the room and swept his gaze over the students with the patented Wexler grin. They beamed back at him and squirmed in their seats. For them the next seven hours couldn't be over fast enough and Wexler echoed their sentiments. It wasn't that this year had been

69

particularly trying or anything; in fact this year's students had been quite the delight. It's just that, after twenty years of teaching, every summer was nicer and nicer when it arrived. It felt like this one was to be the nicest yet. Wexler was going to take a cruise to the Caribbean and live on the beach for a month, courtesy of the rest of his teaching friends who had pooled together the funds to congratulate Wexler on his twenty years of service. It would be a totally off the grid affair, and even though Wexler still loved teaching, he couldn't wait to get away from it all. He was very tempted to start whistling Alice Cooper's "School's Out" but chose to keep it in his head instead. He made his way to his desk at the front of the room still surveying the twenty-six students in his charge, but didn't see the apple on his desk with the pencil sticking out of it until he sat down. It was a big bright red apple, highly polished, with the stem attached and two very green leaves. It appeared to be like everyone's interpretation of your classic apple, the one that would be in every stock image used in every magazine or grocery circular, with the exception of the bright yellow pencil sticking out of it to which there was a note attached. The note was written on paper from a yellow legal pad, torn off at the corner, the writing was in big block letters written with what looked like a red permanent marker. There were four words on the note: "I Fail, You Fail", with the pencil stabbed through the paper at a severe downward angle with most of it buried in the apple. The pencil's eraser had been chewed off with the metal having been bitten down so that it formed a rough blade. Wexler had seen this done to countless pencils before; the boys liked to do it to aid them in "pencil fighting" where they would take turns smacking their pencils against their opponents in attempts to break them, thus making the boy with the intact pencil the winner.

Wexler narrowed his brow as he looked at the apple then looked up at the students. First, he tried to think which one of them put it there, but none had a look of either guilt of a crime or joy of a prank on their faces. His mind went back to the note, "I Fail, You Fail". All of the students had received their final grades the day previous and none of them were failing. Furthermore, he hadn't failed anyone for a couple of years, another source of pride he carried around. He then began to think it was a joke, if not perpetrated by a member of his class, then by a member of another or one of his co-workers. He decided to ask the class directly.

"Well, who do I have to thank for the treat here?" he surveyed. The girl who was always first to class, Amanda Kneupper, and was clearly on the fast track to becoming All-American everything in her high school years, raised her hand.

"Yes, Amanda?"

"It was there when I came in this morning, Mr. Wexler. It looked kind of creepy with the pencil sticking out of it, so I thought it was a joke from someone with an oddball sense of humor." It made sense that one of the other teachers could have slipped it in here before anyone else got in. The janitor unlocked all of the classrooms before most of the staff showed up, so all one had to do was enter before he did, and his arrival time hadn't varied in all his years. He picked up the apple and chucked it into the wastebasket.

"Yeah, it's a joke alright," Wexler said, "just not a very good one."

The rest of the day went uneventfully: the students turned in their text books, Wexler returned a few items of contraband he'd confiscated over the year, the students cleaned out their desks and discussed how exciting it was going to be to actual have lockers the next year at the junior high. The minutes and hours ticked off the clock and finally the last bell rang releasing the students to their summer activities. Some of them were going to camp, some were going on family trips, others just happy to be at home playing endless hours of video games. Wexler had his own visions of beaches and cabana boys dancing in his head at the final bell. But, where the students got to go to their summers immediately, Wexler had about an hour or so before he got to leave then it was straight to the airport. He cleaned out his desk, organized his classroom and gathered a few stray papers here and there. He took the trash to the wastebasket and dumped it. He didn't even notice the apple was gone.

Wexler hopped in his car and drove to the airport. He'd already reserved a space in the long-term lot and made his way there. He parked in his designated spot and hung the tag that gave him permission to park for the entire length of his vacation from the rearview mirror. He took one look at himself in the rearview, flashed his patented grin at himself and then got out of the car to get his one suitcase out of the trunk. He wanted to travel light and pick up anything else he needed once he got to the beach where he'd be staying for the month. He went around to the back of the car, opened the trunk with the key then stood there, dumbfounded, as he saw the apple he'd previously discarded in his classroom now adhered to his leather suitcase with a second pencil adjoining the first that had kept the note in place.

"I Fail, You Fail," the note said. Wexler cocked his head to the side and furrowed his eyebrows again, upset that his bag had been ruined by what was now not just a bad joke but a sick one as well. Wexler reached into the trunk and plucked the apple out, looking at it disgustedly. He looked to his left for a trash can and only saw a sea of cars. He turned to his right to continue his search and was met with a fist to the jaw, knocking him senseless. The apple dropped from his hand and he dropped to the pavement, seeing stars at first and then only black.

Wexler awoke some time later, unsure of how long he had been out. It was dark and he couldn't make out his surroundings. He could only tell he was seated, bound, and had a very foul tasting cloth in his mouth. His jaw hurt from where his assailant/abductor had struck him, and his eyes stinging from the sweat dripping into them. It was hot and humid where his captor had taken him as he strained against his bindings. His legs were bound to the legs of the seat and he could feel his arms were bound together around the back of the chair. He tried to spit the cloth out of his mouth but it, too, was tied tightly and knotted around the backside of his head. He struggled in the chair for a few more minutes then went limp again. He sat there in the darkness. A light came on, beaming directly into his face. The light emanated from a classroom overhead projector, but instead of shining on a screen, it was shining on him. Wexler couldn't see much with the light in his eyes, but he could see someone standing next to the projector. He could also see that he was bound not to a chair but an old school desk. The person next to the projector moved the light a little out of Wexler's eyes, but did not approach; Wexler still couldn't make out who it was. He realized then that this was no longer a joke, that there was probably harm intended for him. The person next to the projector finally addressed him.

"Mr. Wexler. I'm terribly sorry, but I'm afraid your vacation has been cancelled. I need you to attend a session of summer school with me. We're going to be study buddies and then we're going to take a test. Well, I'm going to take the test. You're just going to give me the answers. And the key is if I fail, you fail. See, you already failed me once, but I was the only one that suffered for that. Now, this time if you fail me, you're the one who's going to suffer." The man stepped forward a little but his face was still in shadow. Wexler saw he had the apple in his hands and the man withdrew both of the pencils. He took a bite of the apple, chewed it, then leaned forward so his face was in the light, leering at Wexler. It was the bearded face of Albert Brummer, the school janitor. Brummer leaned in close to Wexler, their faces only a few inches apart.

"I fail, you fail," Brummer said through a mouthful of chewed apple; then spit the contents of his mouth into Wexler's face. Wexler recoiled in revulsion and before he could recover from that horror, Brummer raised one of the pencils high over his head and brought it down into Wexler's right shoulder. Wexler howled in pain against the foul tasting gag in his mouth, the bits of apple dripping off his face immediately forgotten as blood bloomed around the pencil. Brummer walked around to Wexler's left and knelt at his side looking at him.

"I fail, you fail," he repeated, this time driving the remaining pencil into Wexler's left thigh. Wexler screamed into the gag once again at the fresh round of pain and shook in his bindings. Brummer stood up and took another bite of apple as he walked back to the projector. He turned back to Wexler and threw the remains of the apple at his forehead, where it smacked and careened off wildly into the darkness. Wexler didn't feel any pain from the impact, as both his shoulder and thigh were both throbbing loudly. Brummer spun the projector around so it shone on a screen to Wexler's left. From behind the projector, Brummer produced a T.V. set strapped to a wheeled stand which he turned on and positioned in front of Wexler. The screen filled with static and beneath the T.V. was a VCR that constantly flashed 12:00 at him. Brummer then retreated to the back of the darkened room and came back with a box in his hands.

"Ready to study, buddy?" he asked. Wexler could give no reply. Brummer sat the box on top of the T.V. set and reached in to it. He withdrew a VHS tape and inserted it into the VCR. The static screen was filled with an FBI pirating warning then the screen went black after that. The familiar green "Preview" screen came on and Brummer groaned.

"Ugh, previews. Let's just get past this and to the main attraction." He leaned over and pressed the fast forward button to speed up the action on the screen. The green preview screen flashed at least three more times before Brummer hit play and started the tape again. The 1993 film "Tombstone", by George P. Cosmatos, began playing.

"It's my favorite movie," Brummer said. "Be sure to pay close attention and take notes. There may be a quiz later." He burst out laughing and then turned to watch the movie.

Brummer let the tape play all the way through the end of the credits then ejected the tape. He put it back in the box and walked over to Wexler. He reached down and unfastened the knot of the gag on Wexler's mouth, drawing the cloth away.

"Holler if you want, Teach, but you know that's probably pointless, smart as you are. You know I wouldn't be dumb enough to take you anywhere someone would hear you, even though you did think I was dumb enough to fail me." Brummer smacked Wexler across the face with the removed mouth gag and put it in his pocket.

"Ok, Teach, quiz time." Brummer walked over to the overhead projector and placed a transparency on it which was then displayed on the screen. It was a five question quiz, but before Wexler could read any of them, Brummer covered them up with a paper.

"One at a time, Teach. One at a time." He revealed the first question.

"'Who portrayed Doc Holliday in the film?' Ooh, that's easy, I could even answer that one myself," Brummer said. Wexler stayed silent.

"I can't answer these questions without your help, study buddy. Now c'mon...Doc Holliday. Who played him?" Wexler just looked at Brummer then spat defiantly at his feet. Brummer casually walked over and gave a push to the pencil jutting out of his shoulder. Wexler screamed and pulled back as far as his restraints would let him, shouting the answer.

"AAAAAAHHHHHHH! VAL FUCKING KILMER AAAAHHHHHH!!!" Brummer walked over to the projector and withdrew a dry erase marker from his pocket.

"Val...fucking...Kilmer," Brummer muttered as he wrote the answer down on the sheet of plastic. He exposed the second question. "'This famed character actor portrays McMasters'. That might be a tough one."

"Why are you doing this?" Wexler asked. Brummer strode over and grabbed the pencil protruding from Wexler's leg. With a quick motion he snapped off the exposed part of the pencil then jabbed it back into Wexler's leg a few inches away from the initial wound. Wexler rocked against his bindings again, screaming in pain. Brummer was back at the projector, tapping the question with his marker.

"I need an answer here." Wexler gritted his teeth and bit back the pain.

76

"Michael Rooker," he hissed. Brummer wrote his answer on the plastic sheet.

"Alright, next question: What was the first preview before the film?" Brummer looked from the sheet to Wexler, eyebrows raised.

"I can't answer that, you hit fast forward," Wexler moaned. Brummer made an annoyed sound in his throat and rolled his eyes.

"Information comes at you fast, Teach. You gotta be a sponge and soak it all in. Isn't that what you told me?" Wexler recognized his mantra at once; he told it to all his struggling kids. It highlighted his motivational speech when he'd sit them down to talk about their grades. They'd complain about the amount of work, or there was just too much information to absorb, so he'd be supportive and then hit them with the sponge analogy. Now this guy was trying to use it against him.

"I didn't see what it was." Brummer reached in the box on top of the T.V. and produced a pistol. He walked over to Wexler and shot him in the left shoulder.

"Guess," Brummer said flatly. Wexler screamed as the pain from the gunshot superseded the others.

"The 'Burbs! Shit!" Brummer wrote that next to the question on the sheet then revealed the next question.

"Who was County Sheriff when the Earps arrived?"

"Behan," Wexler said, dejectedly. Brummer wrote that on the sheet.

"Final Question. Who was first assistant director on the film?"

"How am I supposed to know that?" Brummer walked over and smacked Wexler in the face.

"We watched the credits, didn't we? First assistant director."

"Dammit, I don't know," Wexler moaned, "John Talbot or something."

"John. Talbot. Or. Something." Brummer said as he wrote. "OK, let's tally up my score." Brummer pulled the sheet of paper away to reveal the answers to the questions.

"Let's see, number one, Val Kilmer, correct. I won't take off any points for his colorful middle name. Number two is indeed Michael Rooker, good job. Number three. Oh man, 'The 'Burbs' is incorrect. The answer should have been 'The Three Musketeers'. Points off for that. Number four, you said Behan. While that's technically correct for the film, in real life the county sheriff of the time was Charles Shibbell."

"But that wasn't in the movie!" Wexler protested.

"So? You're a teacher; you're supposed to know the facts and real history. Not my fault. Points off for that. Number five. The first assistant director was Adam C. Taylor, NOT John Talbot or something. So, two right, three wrong, that's a solid forty percent. Looks like I failed this quiz, study buddy. And you remember what I said, I fail, you fail."

Brummer reached into the box and withdrew a pair of rusty needle nose pliers. He set them on the desk in front of Wexler and then rummaged around in the box again. He withdrew another VHS cassette. This one was a copy of the Ministry "Sphinctour" live album. He popped it in to the VCR and hit fast forward.

"Need to get to the best song," he said over his shoulder to Wexler. "Ah, here it is. N.W.O." He hit play and the video filled the screen. Brummer turned it up to maximum volume. He crossed over to the desk and picked up the pliers. He moved to Wexler's left and put a hand on his forehead, forcing his head back.

"This is going to sting a little bit." Brummer thrust the pliers into Wexler's mouth and latched on to a tooth. He twisted and pulled until he came free with a canine. Wexler howled with pain, barely audible over the loud music. Brummer reached in again and extracted another tooth, this one an incisor. He put the pliers back on the desk, went to the T.V. and turned it off.

"When you failed me, it put me behind a year and behind all of my friends. They got to move on, go to junior high and then high school a year before me. When I got to high school, my friends weren't my friends anymore. They picked on me and ridiculed me for being a freshman when I should have been alongside them, having fun instead of being made fun of. I couldn't take it. I dropped out, left home, left town even. My folks had me declared dead; they barely even looked for me. I had to live off of trash and scraps. I had to take on a different identity because my old one was dead. And then one day, I finally came home. I managed to get a job at the school, using my new persona. And what's one of the first things I see? You. Your twenty year celebration. Your little party, them giving you the gift. And it hit me, it's because of you I was there in the first place, and there you were all smug and self-important and there I was, a bum. Because you failed me."

Brummer turned back and grabbed the rusty pliers, advancing towards Wexler. He grabbed Wexler's right ear and began to pull, Wexler gritted his teeth against the pain and strained once more against his bindings. Through a combination of sweat, blood and force, Wexler's left wrist popped loose from its ropes subsequently freeing his other wrist as well. Brummer hadn't noticed as he was too busy grinning maniacally and pulling on Wexler's ear. Wexler began to feel his skin tear and at that, summoned any and all strength he had and punched Brummer in the gut with a tightly balled left fist. The air went out of Brummer and he doubled over. Wexler took the opportunity and grabbed Brummer's head with both hands, bringing his forehead to meet the desk. There was a loud smack and Brummer reeled backwards and went down on his posterior, cross-eyed and dazed. Wexler frantically pulled at the bindings on his ankles and managed to free himself from the desk. He stood up, but fresh pain from the pencil wounds nearly brought him to his knees. He looked over to the fallen Brummer, who had now rolled over to all fours and was attempting to stand. With a cry that was equal parts pain, frustration and rage, Wexler charged at the mounted T.V. set and toppled it over on to Brummer, stand and all. It hit him square in the back and forced him to the floor with an audible "OOPH!", while both the T.V. and VCR came loose from the straps holding them. Brummer struggled under the cart and managed to flip over, trying to get out from underneath the thing. He pushed off the cart and began looking around wildly for his gun. Wexler picked up the VCR and called to Brummer.

"Hey, dumb shit. Catch." He threw the VCR at Brummer who just blinked at it and then blocked it with the bridge of his nose. He roared with pain and anger and his nose gushed blood. Forgetting the gun, he put his hands underneath himself to try to push off and stand to face his once captor, now combatant. Wexler, meanwhile, had picked up the T.V.

"Uh-uh, fella, you stay down. I pass, YOU FAIL!" Wexler raised the T.V. over his head and brought it down with a sickening crunch on top of Brummer's cranium as an exclamation point to his statement. The janitor twitched and flopped around for a minute before finally ceasing and laying still. Wexler saw the gun a few feet away from Brummer's body, where it had fallen after the initial struggle. Wexler walked over and picked it up, studying it for a few seconds before turning it on Brummer's prone body and emptying the clip in to it, thinking the whole time, "Fuck that, I've seen this movie."

The Drummer

It is said that Robert Johnson once stood at The Crossroads and signed a deal with the devil that gave him amazing talent as a bluesman. The fact that he had talent was undeniable. The recordings that have survived back up this truth, but what is less known to history and recorded time is whether Johnson actually met *El Diablo* at said Crossroads and signed said pact in ink, blood or otherwise. Robert Johnson died young taking every truth he knew about anything with him, leaving behind only legends, recordings of his music and conjecture. His death at the age of twenty-seven also established him with other rare company: The 27 Club, a long list of musicians who, for one reason or another, by their own hand or another's, met their end at the age of twenty-seven. The list includes (but is definitely not limited to) Jim Morrison, Jimi Hendrix, Janis Joplin, Mia Zapata, Kurt Cobain, Amy Winehouse, Jacob Miller and Johnson himself. There is speculation in some circles that the pact with the devil and the demise at the age of twenty-seven are linked, related somehow; that the deal comes due when the musician turns that age or soon thereafter. This would have to mean that some of the greatest and most revered musical performers from across the ages were either Satanists, or had made deals with Satan which sounds absolutely ludicrous when you say it out loud. Maybe Johnson was alone in his deals with the devil. The rest of the 27 Club is just a very unfortunate coincidence where so many up and coming musicians all just happened to kick off at a certain age. I can't speak for them or for Johnson. I can only tell you of what I went through.

I've been around music my entire life. My dad was a roadie for Motley Crue in the 80's where he met my mom, one of Vince Neil's castoffs. My Pop always said the pay was alright, but the fringe benefits were out-of-this-world. Anyhow, my mom died of an overdose when I was only two, so I only know what my Pop tells me of her. After she passed, I went on the road with him and one of my first clear memories is of Tommy Lee doing a sound check before a show in Tampa. I remember watching in quiet awe as this man flailed away, seemingly at random, on his drum kit and produced the most cohesive sounds. That was when I fell in love with the drums.

I swiped a pair of Tommy's drumsticks later in the tour and started flailing away at random. I wasn't any good. To see it would have been to see some little kid banging away on anything that would produce a sound. My Pop saw me one day and got me my own mini drum kit so I could practice. I think he also did it so I wouldn't keep banging on random things and causing more damage than the band did in their hotel rooms. Anyway, I had something to practice on, and I finally started to get better. Tommy even came by a couple of times and gave me a few pointers, teaching me how to make a bass drum sound like a double bass, little things like that. I practiced pretty much every day on that little kit, so much so that I beat it to death. I had already splintered more than a few sticks along the way, and that little kit was a trooper. Finally one day, it could take no more and fell apart. I was distraught. That kit felt like my only friend sometimes out on the road. Sure, my Pop was there with me, but he was usually busy during the day setting up shows (or tearing them down at night). The day my kit fell apart, I was really in a playing mood. I'd constructed this little two minute solo that I wanted to show my Pop later that day, and now with no drums, I couldn't do that. All of the band's equipment was on stage and Tommy's drum kit was already assembled. I slipped on stage since it was lunch hour and all the roadies and sound men were at the catering area. I got behind Tommy's kit and marveled at the size of it. I sat in his chair and lowered it so I could reach the kick pedals. There was a pair of sticks on the snare drum. I picked them up and tried to twirl them like I'd seen Tommy do. They went flying out of my hands and clattered to the floor. I retrieved them and, though I would get the twirling down pat much later, I didn't attempt to do it again. Instead, I tapped the snare and the hi-hat cymbal trying to get a feel of the huge kit. I dropped my foot on the bass pedal a couple of times, and then launched into my little solo. The sound of the kit being played brought my Pop and the rest of the roadies running. They skidded to a stop and watched as this five year old kid jammed on Tommy Lee's drum kit. I still use that little solo to this day.

In retrospect, I still wasn't very good but my Pop and the guys all applauded when I was done. I was so lost in my playing that I didn't know they were there. I was expecting a harsh punishment from my old man for playing Tommy's drums in the first place, but the only discipline I got was a brand new full sized drum kit. It was nowhere near the size of Tommy's: a bass drum, snare drum, tom-tom, hi-hat, ride and crash cymbals and a cowbell. Many years later, I saw a skit on Saturday Night Live with Christopher Walken saying he had a fever and the only prescription was more cowbell. If he'd have been around when I was playing, he'd have O.D.'ed on cowbell. I loved the way it sounded, that hollow "Tonk! Tonk! Tonk!", which I could use it to keep time and give me some rest when my arms got tired.

After a couple of years on the road, my old man decided to put us in a more permanent place. We got a modest house right outside of L.A. and I started to attend regular school. I still practiced my drumming every day: we set up the kit in the unused garage and my Pop soundproofed the walls so as not to disturb the non-rocking neighbors. I made a couple of friends at school, but that drum kit was my best friend of all. I'd come home, do my homework and go straight out to the garage. Most days, it just felt good to get out there and play. Some days it was a way to relieve stress or deal with a bad day. I mean, what friend would let you beat on him all day and still be there tomorrow? None. That's why my drum kit became my best friend, my shoulder to cry on, and my ear to talk to. When I got to high school, I didn't try out to be in band, their brand of music wasn't what I was into, and I didn't want to be labeled a band geek. I was listening to Napalm Death, Godflesh and Cannibal Corpse. As such, I hung around with the rest of the metal-heads; none of those guys would be caught dead in a band uniform. Some of the guys would come over to my house after school. We'd hang out in the garage and smoke cigarettes and a little pot. I'd play and they'd listen. Between junior and senior year I had to attend summer school to make up a class that I hadn't done too well in. That's when I met Danny Bippert, a cat as smooth as glass and just as sharp. He came over to my house one day and listened to me play. He asked if I'd ever thought of starting a band. I told him I didn't know anybody who played. He borrowed my phone and called a couple of guys he knew, Jack Freeman and Freddy Winthrop. I knew *of* them from our circle of metal-heads, but didn't really *know* them. They showed up with a couple of guitars and amps and we had an impromptu jam session right there. Danny said he didn't have any musical talent, but he showed me some of his writing and I told him I thought we could turn some of them into songs. The Psychedelic Tadpoles were born that day and I was in my first band.

We didn't stay as a band very long, but that summer jamming with those guys was fun. I knew this is what I wanted to do for the rest of my life. I did some research on other famous drummers, which there are surprisingly few of. I read up on Neal Pert, Phil Collins and others. I knew that starting a successful band as just a drummer would be difficult; there had been few people who had done the double duty as drummer and front man. Instead I scoured the music rags for bands seeking drummers, or guys who wanted to start bands from the ground up. I found a couple from both camps, did a few auditions but got no callbacks. I graduated school and when I couldn't find steady work, my Pop reached out to a few of his music contacts and got me a gig doing studio sessions for some local acts. I also played for a couple of commercial jingles. It was good enough money, but I wanted to be on stage in front of the screaming fans. I wanted to be able to throw my sticks out in to the sea of humanity that was the mosh pit and have somebody catch my stick and cherish it. That was never going to happen while I was stuck in the studio, a nameless, faceless percussionist.

One day a few weeks after my twentieth birthday, I laid down a drum track for some new energy beverage at the studio. I was walking home when I caught a whiff of what smelled like lit matches. I didn't pay much attention to it, it was just another in the myriad of smells I encountered on a daily basis. The only thing that struck me as odd was that the wind was blowing into my face, yet the smell seemed to be coming from behind me. I turned around, but there was no one there. That was as much thought as I gave the matter, until later when I smelled it again, but this time a man accompanied it. He was sharply dressed with very shiny shoes. He had a large chin with a finely groomed goatee pointing out of it. I guessed my Pop had let him in and shown him into the garage. All I know is, I was playing and then I could smell him. In the still air of the garage the sulfur smell just hung there, not like when I was outside and had smelled it on the breeze. It hung around this guy, like he'd spent a few hours in a sulfur pit and the stench had clung to him. I smelled him and stopped playing, looking in the direction of the smell and then my eyes locked on to his. He was smiling a tight-lipped grin and was leaning against the wall with his arms crossed over his chest. For a second I thought I recognized him from the days on the road with my Pop. In fact, I was almost sure of it. I had seen this guy somewhere before, but I couldn't come up with either a city or a venue. He unfolded his arms and waved his hand at me, making the universal "Keep Going" gesture, and then refolded his arms over his chest. I thought to myself that this guy must be one of my Pop's music contacts, like the one who had gotten me the studio job. So, in an effort to impress, I broke into my best Lars Ulrich impression and played the drum-line for Metallica's "One". When I finished, dripping sweat from places I didn't know I could sweat from, his tight-lipped grin broke into a wide one. He clapped his long fingered hands together in applause, a large ring glinting in the dim light of the garage. Every time he brought his hands together, that ring reflected light into my eyes and suddenly I knew this guy was here to help me. He complemented my playing and said he hadn't seen skills like that in a while. I thanked him and said I wished my skills were good enough to make the big time. He smiled even wider and said that was precisely why he was there. He explained he was putting a group together and, that since he felt the drums were the backbone to every song, was looking for a drummer first. He approached me at the drum kit and withdrew a piece of paper from inside his jacket. I thought I had gotten used to his smell, but as he drew closer it got stronger and I winced away from it. He must have noticed, because he pulled a spritzer bottle from another jacket pocket and hit himself with a few sprays of the liquid inside. The air filled with the scent of patchouli oil. He placed the spritzer back in his jacket pocket and turned his attention to the paper. He explained that it was just a standard contract, good for seven years and would I be interested. I asked him how much his cut was. I don't know much about contract law, but I know one had to be careful in these arrangements or you could get saddled with a deal like Elvis had or The Beatles to a lesser extent. He told me he had a small finder's fee; that all profits and royalties would go to the band. His interests lie in making a successful band, not make it rich. I told him it all seemed a little too good to be true, everybody was out to make a buck these days and usually off someone else's back. He explained he was already a rich man, money held no allure for him. His passion was music and getting more of it out there. I liked his way of thinking, I told him. He smiled that wide grin of his and thrust the paper at me. I asked him where he was going to get the other musicians from; he told me he was going to leave that up to me. He would have say-so over the final product, but he wanted

89

me to choose musicians instead of having them foisted upon me. Creates a better vibe and harmony, he said. I took the paper from him and gave it a quick scan. Like I said, I'm no contract law expert, and, unfortunately, I was also one of those types of people who just scrolled to the end of any user agreement and checked the "I Agree" box without hesitation, just to get on with the damn thing. I should have read the contract.

I signed the paper and handed it back to him. It disappeared inside the jacket of the sharply dressed man with the really shiny shoes. His wide smile turned into a rictus grin and he arched his eyebrows at me. He reminded me of The Joker from Batman: The Animated Series, the one voiced by Mark Hamill. And then his face returned to normal and I questioned whether I really saw it at all, like maybe the shadows just played with his face for a second. He had returned to the spot in the room where I first saw him, leaning on the wall again. He asked if I took requests. I laughed and said "Sure". He wanted to hear "Don't Fear the Reaper" by Blue Oyster Cult, said to not spare on the cowbell. Then he knelt down to a guitar case on the floor, one that I hadn't previously noticed. He told me it was only an acoustic, but he'd get me started with the opening riff. Now, I'd heard plenty of BOC with my old man around, he loved them. I was super familiar with "Don't Fear the Reaper" but had never played it before. But as soon as the sharply dressed man hit the opening riffs of the song, I knew just where to come in and what to hit and when to hit it. I drummed the living shit out of that song and I did not spare the cowbell. I finished playing and when I was done, only then did I notice I was alone in the garage again, a faint hint of patchouli still in the air.

I went to the studio the next day, the sharply dressed man with the really shiny shoes was there. I had called Danny Bippert the night before and told him to meet me there. He showed up about ten minutes after I did. I told him what I was doing and that I wanted to get the old band back together. The sharply dressed man stood across the room and said nothing, just nodded in what I assumed was approval. Danny called Jack and Freddy up and got them down to the studio. We set our equipment up and went through a few of the old tunes, and did a couple of covers like "Ace of Spades" by Motorhead and "Sober" by Tool. Each song felt better than the last and we were all having fun. The sharply dressed man in the really shiny shoes applauded loudly after each one and at the end of the day we felt we really might have something here. The sharply dressed man said he was going to get us a gig booked to see how we did in front of an audience. We thought he meant some little club or something. We found out two days later that we were playing at the Whisky-A-Go-Go. For our first gig. The Psychedelic Tadpoles were back in a big way.

We practiced every day up to the show, still not believing our luck. We decided to change our name: Fat Guy Falling was the front runner for a long while, then we were The Lebowski's (Danny's favorite movie was "The Big Lebowski"), and then for about five minutes (after a particularly heavy pot smoking session) we were Dick McPlenty and The Swinging Cox. We finally settled on Devil's Advocate. We all agreed it had a natural feel and started to throw around ideas for album covers. The day of the show, we asked the sharply dressed man who we'd be playing with, and he said the stage would be all ours. There would be a club full of people there to see just us. I asked the sharply dressed man if he was going to be there, and he said no, that he had other matters to attend to. Danny was starting to get nervous, so I told him he should do like Jim Morrison did when he started out and have his back to the crowd until he got over his stage fright. Danny said he'd be all right;

he'd just need a drink or two before going on. We pulled up to the Whisky in Danny's truck with our gear and set it up. We did a quick sound check and went backstage to get Danny ready for his first public performance. We went onstage at nine o' clock. We played all of our originals, with covers of "Jerry Was a Racecar Driver" by Primus and Metallica's "Battery" sprinkled in there. Danny owned the stage as soon as we started our first song, stage fright nothing but a footnote. Our set lasted about an hour and a half; we came out to do an encore and brought the house down with a cover of Pantera's "Cowboys from Hell". We were barely offstage when the club manager came running up to us and asked when we could come back. I wanted to direct him to the sharply dressed man in the really shiny shoes who'd handled our previous booking, but I didn't have a number or a card. Hell, I suddenly realized that I didn't know his name.

I got to the studio the next day intent on asking the sharply dressed man in the really shiny shoes some questions, but he wasn't there. Instead, there was another fellow. He introduced himself as Gerry Westly. He told me he had been hired as the band's manager, had already spoken to the manager of The Whisky and we were booked for the next month as the house band. I couldn't believe it. As the house band, we'd be opening for all the big name acts that rolled through there. You couldn't pay for exposure like that as a fledgling band just starting out, yet here we were getting paid for the exposure! I asked him how much of our cut he was getting and he informed me he had been paid a nominal fee; that he wouldn't receive anything from what we earned. I got the rest of the guys to the studio and filled them in; they were as stunned as I was. We decided right then to start working on new material, so we could have at least two new songs for our next show. Danny had this hilarious song written about drinking all night and spending up your paycheck, only to wake up next to a fat girl in the morning. He said he drew from personal experience to create it. We all howled with laughter! I came up with a sick drum line, Freddy developed the bass, and Jack came in with the guitar riff. After just a couple of minutes, we knew we had the meat of the song. We ran through it one more time, this time Danny joined in with the vocals.

There I was at the bar,

Drank up half my check.

This chick walks up and grabs my ass

And kisses on my neck.

Drank some more, took her home

Started to make out.

Put my hand up her skirt

And pulled her panties down.

(Chorus)

A tit in my left hand,

A tit in my right.

I fucked her cunt and then her butt

And then I said good night.

She goes down, my pants do too

She starts to give me head.

We tumble down to the couch

Instead of to the bed.

(Chorus)

Then I got that feeling,

I told her to watch out.

I pulled it out and then popped off

It hit her in the mouth.

Rolled over in the morning

Caught myself a sight.

300 pounds of human flab

What did I do last night?

(Chorus)

We made it through in one take, but it was difficult because we were laughing so hard. Danny didn't have a title for it; it was something he had scribbled down in his notebook. I came up with the title, "Blind on Satan's Sauce"; a euphemism for beer-goggles. All four of us were extremely pleased with it and decided we would close our first show with it. As for a second new song, Jack had this crunching guitar riff he'd been working on and Freddy found a low doom sounding bass riff to pair with it. I threw in a double bass drum with plenty of snare drum and crash cymbal to get this aggressive beat going. It sounded like an angry song, so Danny started freestyling some lyrics to it. He came up with a guy beating up another guy, like really kicking his ass. We liked this one almost as much as the previous song one and gave this one the title "Fight Song". We ran through a couple of other tunes, did a cover of "Young Men Dead" by The Black Angels and called it a day. It had been such a fun and productive day that I had forgotten about all the things I had meant to ask the sharply dressed man in the really shiny shoes.

The day of the gig arrived quickly; we'd had one more practice in the meantime and were ready to take the stage. The club had us opening for Internet Scum that night. We were determined that all their fans would leave as ours that night. We took the stage around eight o' clock and put on a forty-five minute set. The crowd was in to it and we got a good sized pit going. When we played "Fight Song" the people went nuts, really feeling the energy of the song, but when we played "Blind on Satan's Sauce" to close our set they all kind of stopped and listened. You could tell they were into it, sure, but they were also absorbing it. When we finished they ERUPTED. We knew these people would be telling their friends about us the next day. We got off the stage and when we got backstage, Dak, lead singer for Internet Scum, gave us hearty congrats and said he'd loved every minute of it, but that last song was total insanity. He'd never heard a crowd react like that to a song before, not even any of theirs. We put all our gear away positively beaming, and then we went back into the club to celebrate the rest of the night and enjoy our recent success. We were mobbed as soon as we got back inside! We managed to get ourselves a table and proceeded to not pay for a drink the rest of the night. Each one of the guys had a girl, or three, draped over them (I had one myself), and all manner of people were coming up to us and clapping us on the back and saying how awesome the set was, the final song most of all. Most of our crowd of people even hung around when Internet Scum hit the stage. Devil's Advocate had arrived.

The next day, I was nursing a hangover when Gerry Westly called. He needed me down at the studio to check out some offers. He told me there had been some record company execs in the club the previous night, and they were all fighting for the rights to our first album. I showered up and went to the studio, the rest of the guys were already there. Each one of us was in worse shape than the other, but we were all excited to get this venture underway. We listened to several pitches and then conferred as a band with our manager. We went with a four album deal from Cold Claw Records and it was worth a princely sum. We signed the necessary documents and then, after the deal was done, proceeded to work on our next hangover. We left the studio and went around the corner to McGee's, a little pub run by a crusty old Irish dude. We had some shots and toasted each other with beers and enjoyed the night; tomorrow would be day one of recording the new album, regardless of how we felt. Midway through the night I got up to hit the pisser and when I got there, the two urinals were occupied, but the sit-down toilet was open, so I went into the stall and shut the door. I was halfway through relieving myself when I smelled that smell of matches again; I thought somebody had probably lit some to cover a particularly rancid fart or something. I finished up, flushed and exited the stall. The sharply dressed man in the really shiny shoes was standing there, the rest of the room was empty even though I'd heard no one enter or exit the bathroom the entire time I'd been in the stall. I nodded at the sharply dressed man in the really shiny shoes and approached the sink to wash up, feeling a little uneasy. He talked to my back, congratulating me on the record deal and heaping praise on us. I washed my hands and thanked him, and then I stood up and looked at his reflection in the mirror. I could see that he was just as sharply dressed as ever, and his shoes had an impossible shine to them, but where his head and hands should have been there was nothing but angry red fire. The flames leapt and jumped and twisted. The sharply dressed man in the really shiny shoes also cast a shadow on the wall in the reflection, one that was dark black and endless. You knew if that shadow ever crossed you that you would fall into it and be lost forever. I turned around to face him, hands wet, but he was just as normal looking as ever, casually leaning up against the wall with that wide-mouthed grin, hands clasped together in front of him. He pulled a couple hand towels out of the dispenser and handed them to me, his rings glinting in the dim bathroom light. I took the towels from him, hardly noticing how warm they were.

Recording the album went smoothly. We chose "Fight Song" to open, followed by eleven more tracks, with "Blind on Satan's Sauce" closing it out. We had one cover song on the album, a really heavy take on Madonna's "Like a Virgin". That one we had come up with one day in the studio when we were talking about how a few bands had done covers of 80's songs and put their spin on it, either speeding it up or changing the genre entirely. We tossed around examples like Marilyn Manson's version of Eurythmics' "Sweet Dreams (Are Made of This)" and Alien Ant Farm doing Michael Jackson's "Smooth Criminal", so we decided to do one of our own.

We wanted it to be a little tongue-in-cheek, though, to poke fun at it while taking it seriously all the same, so we needed a song that would be ridiculous for us to cover in the first place. The ideas we first tossed around were "The Promise" by When in Rome, "All Out of Love" by Air Supply, and "Enola Gay" by Orchestral Manoeuvres in the Dark. Then Danny said we do "Like a Virgin" and we all agreed that was just ridiculous enough. It took us roughly three weeks to cut all the songs for the album, and then Gerry turned it over to our producer. We named the album "The Opening Salvo" and set about choosing artwork for the cover. We looked at pictures of D-Day and the storming of Normandy; eventually we found a picture of American soldiers charging up the beach with explosions going off around them. It was perfect. The entire time we maintained our gig at The Whisky and built up more of a following. Finally, the album was done, packaged and ready for release. We had the release party at The Whisky, naturally, and of course we were the headliners that night with the place packed. It was a raucous show and we had a fantastically hedonistic time. All copies of the album we brought with us sold out. We felt it was time to put together a tour.

Once our gig at The Whisky came to its conclusion, we were free to hit the road. Gerry had gotten us spots on a couple of tours; we weren't quite ready to headline our own tour just yet. We needed more national exposure to be able to do that. So we played a couple of festivals, and opened on a few other tours. Each show our merchandise booth sold out of our album, and usually shirts, too. We gathered enough steam over the next seven months that we were finally able to book a fifteen date tour of our own. During all of this, our album had sold out of its first printing, so a second printing was ordered by the record company. Our album was being stocked by the national record chains, and it seemed they couldn't get enough. The record company had released "Like a Virgin" as a single, with "Blind on Satan's Sauce" as a b-side. "Like a Virgin" was getting heavy radio play, and its b-side was a huge underground hit. It was too vulgar to get played on the radio, but it gained in popularity, regardless. We added ten more dates to the tour, and then to close out the year, we played a New Year's bash at The Whisky.

We started the New Year in the studio, writing and recording the follow-up to "The Opening Salvo". We already had a huge tour scheduled for later that spring to support the new album, so we were under a deadline to get it finished and in stores. We took it all in stride, however, and felt the songs come to us effortlessly. The second album was also thirteen tracks, like the first, and featured some of the heaviest stuff we'd done yet. We wanted this album to have a darker tone than the last, so there were no funny songs, or tongue-in-cheek 80's covers. All the tunes on this one were originals, and the only cohesiveness between them is that they were all fast and heavy. We drew on early Slayer and Metallica for inspiration, but with a little more emphasis on the bass this time. The public ate it up and bought this album just as greedily, if not more so, than the last. The supporting tour sold out; we were a bona fide success. It felt like we could do no wrong. We made appearances on some late night talk shows, then we got the call from Saturday Night Live. We wanted to do "Blind on Satan's Sauce" but they said there was no way to censor it enough to go on live TV. Instead we got to perform "Like a Virgin" and a cut off of the new album, "Futility". Colin Farrell was the host of that night's episode; he came up to us after the show and wanted our autographs on his albums. That blew my mind.

Over the next several years, we experienced unparalleled success. We went on to make the next two albums to fulfill our contract with Cold Claw, then signed a new four album deal with them, worth twice as much as the previous deal. Our shows sold out domestically and overseas, and the albums did just as well. We had throngs of fans wherever we went; and our pick of the women in them.

Three months after my twenty-seventh birthday, we were scheduled to play a gig in Sturgis, South Dakota during the first week of August for the Bike Rally. I had recently purchased a motorcycle and made a bit of news for actually riding it to the rally from our last gig across country, unlike a lot of the participants who ship their bikes and fly in. Gerry hemmed and hawed about it, saying it was a risk, and if I got hurt or killed...blah, blah, blah. So we decided to make a bit of bigger news out of it and when I got to the rally I'd just ride up on stage for the beginning of our set. We figured it would be a cool stunt and the crowd would go nuts. I was about an hour out from where the show was, and I stopped off to take a piss before I got to the show and would be onstage for the next hour and a half or so. It was a dusty little gas station, but the men's room was unlocked and clean and that was a welcome sight in a world of so many shat upon toilet seats. I finished my business and flushed with my foot (can't be too careful), and turned to exit the stall. Leaning against the wall in front of the open door was the man in the really shiny shoes. He was picking at his fingernails and not looking at me; legs crossed as he leaned against the wall. He muttered that it was time to collect on our contract, still not looking at me. I asked him what he meant, and he said that it was all there in the fine print. I told him I didn't know what fine print he was talking about. He then looked at me with his rictus grin spreading into a shark's maw before howling that nobody ever reads the fine print. Seven years of success his toothy face screamed at me, as he unfurled the paper I signed, producing it from nowhere; in exchange for my soul. He held the paper in my face, and there was the fine print, disguised as the line that I signed my name on. He withdrew the paper and it disappeared, and I didn't see where, nor did I care. I felt weak in my legs and I pushed past him, going out of the bathroom and in to the sunlight. I heard him call after me, telling me to enjoy the show.

I got on my bike and rode the rest of the way to the show, and when I got there I told the guys I didn't feel like doing the stunt anymore, and went to my dressing room. I sat in a chair and put my head in my hands. When I looked up, he was standing there in his really shiny shoes, a soft look on his face. He told me to go enjoy my last show; that he'd collect when I was finished. He wanted to hear me play one last time, he said. I got up, grabbed my sticks and joined the guys backstage. They took no notice of my lack of enthusiasm; we were introduced and took the stage to a huge ovation. We played an hour and a half set, doing all the fan favorites and a couple of covers. All the while I saw the sharply dressed man in the really shiny shoes standing at the back of the crowd; hands behind his back and smiling at me. The final song of the set was going to be "Blind on Satan's Sauce" and as we started the song, I noticed the man in the shiny shoes start to make his way toward the stage through the crowd. He wasn't pushing or forcing his way through, though, people were just getting out of his way subconsciously. We played the song and the mosh pit went crazy and the man in the shiny shoes kept coming towards me. I heard Danny's singing and noticed he was on the last line before the last chorus. I looked at Jack and Freddy as they wailed away on their machines. I felt my face start to get hot and I hit the skins even harder. I looked at the crowd, and the sharply dressed man in the really shiny shoes was standing directly in front of the stage, the crowd dancing around him. He looked up at me and nodded. The song ended, but I kept on drumming.

FROM THE AUGUST 12TH EDITION OF ROLLING STONE MAGAZINE:

Casey Atkins, 27, Drummer for Devil's Advocate, Dies Onstage

By: Melissa Randle

Tragedy struck the Sturgis Black Hills Motorcycle Rally earlier this week as Casey Atkins, drummer for popular rock group Devil's Advocate, passed away at the age of 27 while the band was finishing up its set at the rally. According to witnesses, the band was playing its underground hit "Blind on Satan's Sauce" as their show closer, when at the end of the song, Atkins kept furiously playing his drum set. Seemingly putting on a solo performance for the ages, Atkins reportedly kept playing for about six minutes relentlessly before collapsing on to his drum set. Attempts to revive him onstage were unsuccessful and he was pronounced dead on the scene by local authorities. Cause of death is undetermined as of this time pending a full autopsy and toxicological screening.

Best Buds

The families of James "Jimmy" McCoy and Joseph "Joey" Cavanaugh moved to the same street, to two adjacent houses, only weeks apart. Jimmy's family arrived first, in the middle of July, then Joey's family settled in right before the start of school in August. Due to the hectic, whirlwind schedule of moving, unpacking and preparing for the school year, neither of the new neighbors had time to meet each other and their respective families, so the boys wouldn't get to make acquaintance until the first day of school. Both boys were six years old and due to begin their second grade classes and would finally come face-to-face while waiting for the school bus. Both were nervous as hell: they were both the "new kid", didn't know anybody, and in a whole new town. This helped to form the bond between them, there on that street curb. They became inseparable from that point on.

They came to find out from each other that their birthdays were only a week apart, Joey was the older, but he never ribbed Jimmy about it or rubbed it in his face. They both really dug "The Transformers" and thought "The Go-Bots" were lame. They both loved the New York Yankees and Don Mattingly, who was having a decent year even if The Yanks weren't. They both collected Spider-Man comic books, and if one boy had an issue the other didn't, he would graciously let his buddy read it, but only in his room, of course. One of the only things they couldn't agree upon was that Jimmy was a Matchbox guy, and Joey was a Hot Wheels man. This always made for spirited conversation, which led up to "Raceday Sunday": tracks were built and drag races held between the fastest each company had to offer. It usually ended in a dead heat, but every once in a while there would be a victor, who would have bragging rights for precisely twenty-three hours before the next debate began and the next competitors would be chosen.

When they were eight, they discovered WWF wrestling and became raging Hulkamaniacs. Everything became 24 inch Pythons-this, and "Say your prayers, eat your vitamins"-that. Red and yellow bandannas were worn around the house with nary a care, and there were two mini-Hogans running around the neighborhood at Halloween that year. They would practice the big boot and leg-drop combo on each other, with each boy "Hulking-out" and kicking out of the ref's three count at the last second. But as is often, new champions emerge and new heroes are created, so the following year, the colors shifted from red and yellow to pink and black. Bret "The Hitman" Hart was who the boys looked up to, and would spend endless hours perfecting "The Sharpshooter" on each other. The year after that it was "The Heartbreak Kid" Shawn Michaels and "Sweet Chin Music", then "The Undertaker" and "The Tombstone Piledriver".

When they were thirteen, they discovered girls and shopping malls; one usually came with the other. They would ride their bikes to the mall with a pocket full of quarters for the video game arcade, pen and paper for girls' phone numbers. The paper would remain as empty at the end of the day as it was in the beginning, pen remaining capped. The girls were plentiful; the boys' courage was not. Then, in the summer of their fourteenth year, Jimmy managed to strike up a conversation at the food court with a girl while her friends were still in line at the Sbarro. By the time they had returned to her, he had gotten her number, the paper finally written on, the pen finally uncapped. Jimmy actually ended up handing the girl's number over to Joey, it was him that she was interested in, after all, but Jimmy didn't mind. The seal had been broken and Jimmy felt he had all the confidence in the world to approach any girl at the food court from now on.

When they were fifteen, the boys discovered marijuana. Joey had moved on to other girls since the initial one at the mall, as had Jimmy, they were both veterans at "number getting" now. The next phone number they would get at the mall, however, did not belong to a girl. Martin Proctor was an older kid from the school that they knew of, but didn't really know. They knew he was a kid that regularly had detention, and went across the street at lunch time to smoke cigarettes with some of the other older kids. Jimmy and Joey saw him often at the arcade at the mall, though he was never playing any games, just walking around and talking to the other kids. Sometimes Martin and another kid would go outside, and then

Martin would come back alone, with the other kid following about ten minutes later, grinning and red-eyed. One day, out of the blue, Martin approached the boys and talked them up.

"Sup, fellas. Wanna get high?" Martin asked.

"What's that?" Jimmy asked in reply.

"It's where we smoke this joint, and everything gets better."

"Isn't that illegal?" Joey inquired.

"That's half the fun, my man. Burn this, get happy and stick it to the man," Martin said with a smile. "Besides, it's only illegal because the big, bad government can't figure out the best way to regulate it. It's all natural, grown in nature, and picked by hard working people trying to make a living. What's bad about that?" Joey and Jimmy nodded at each other in agreement and followed Martin outside. They went to the big ditch behind the mall where all the skaters liked to hang out and try to be the next Tony Hawk or Bob Burnquist. The three boys sat on the concrete embankment and Martin sparked up the joint. He dragged deeply and passed it to Jimmy who looked at it once more, then at Joey.

"Point of no return," Jimmy said. He put the joint to his lips and dragged on it like a cigarette, then started coughing wildly as soon as he inhaled the smoke. Martin hooted with laughter.

"Gotta cough to get off, man!" he said, clapping Jimmy on the back. Jimmy passed the hooter to Joey, who sucked the weed smoke straight into his lungs. He started to cough, but stifled it and kept the smoke in. Martin looked impressed.

"Whew, look at this guy...looks like a natural," Martin complimented.

"I seen my sister doing it in the back yard one time," Joey said while exhaling. "Told her I'd keep quiet if she gave me her tips from the diner for a week."

When the boys were eighteen, they discovered the real world when they graduated high school. They both already had jobs working at a local fast food joint. They decided to move out of their parent's houses and get a place of their own, which they quickly realized was not going to be easy on two fast food salaries. They both decided to take some classes at the community college, with Joey studying auto repair and Jimmy learning welding. After completing their respective courses, they were able to find jobs that were more lucrative salary wise, while they decided to look to the future and started planning a car repair and customization shop. By the time they had turned twenty-one, they had enough money saved to rent a location, get equipment and open the shop. With their business model in hand, they went to the bank and secured a small business loan, which they used to by a few cars to make some show pieces for the business. With that, J & J Customs was born.

With much of their daily lives entrenched in making the business succeed, the boys began to realize that they didn't have much of a social life. They agreed to pull back from the business at least once a week to cut loose and have some fun, maybe meet a lady or two. The very first time they went out, Joey hooked up with a stunning blonde named Tricia. She was new in town, but had heard of the shop, and was all over Joey when she heard he was part owner. Said she loved hot rods and going fast and would Joey take her out in his fastest ride. Joey was smitten, of course, and fell for her hard. They dated for about seven months, Joey built her a car, and Jimmy would put up with the sex noises whenever she stayed overnight because his friend was happy. It was around this time that the

Lakeland Car Show was going on, and the boys had entered one of their customs in the Low-rider competition. They didn't win the competition, they actually managed fourth place, but a collector at the show had taken a shine to the vehicle, and offered to buy it from the boys on the spot. They agreed, and made a handsome $10,000 profit when all was said and done. Since their car hadn't placed third or higher, it wasn't in the running for Car of the Show, and since they didn't own it anymore, they decided to leave a day early. Jimmy dropped Joey off at their apartment; Joey said he was going to grab his car and head to Tricia's for a little welcome home gift a day early. Jimmy said he was going to head to the shop and check on some things, he was there when Joey called him.

"It's over, man. That bitch was lubing up someone else's undercarriage," Joey said flatly.

"Tricia? What happened, bro?"

"Came in her front door as Larry Jenkins came in her back door."

"Larry Jenkins? The stockboy from the Sac-n-Pac?"

"The very same. Although I'm sure he prefers 'Stock-man'. He didn't look like much of a 'boy'. That guy was hung like a Clydesdale."

"What happened then?"

"Well, there was a bunch of swearing and clothes flying around, so I didn't get much in the confusion. Best I could tell was that I spend too much time in the shop and not enough time in her. Hence her riding the Clydesdale like she was trying to win the Kentucky Derby."

"Shit, man, I'm sorry. Can I do anything, what do you need?"

"Don't worry 'bout me, man, I'm gonna take the one chick out who's never done me wrong and drive around a while with her. Me and Mary Jane are gonna have a session." Joey hung up and Jimmy waited a day before going out to look for his friend. He looked at three of four places he thought Joey would go and, when he didn't find him there, he knew Joey would be at the fourth place.

Jimmy found Joey at the drag-strip, sitting on the hood of his car. Joey was smoking a joint, Nazareth's version of "Love Hurts" pouring out of the car's speakers. Jimmy walked up to him and put a hand on his shoulder.

"Hey, man, you alright?" Jimmy asked.

"Eh, I 'spose. She's not the first one to break up with me, probably won't be the last. Chicks, man. They're always so damn complicated. Remember when we were kids, man, and we didn't have to worry about 'em. It was just me and you and shit was just so *simple.* Our biggest concern was fucking Hot Wheels and stupid Matchbox." Joey flicked the roach to the roadway after one long drag.

"Yeah. Raceday Sunday. I think I still have some tracks in my mom's garage. Cars, too."

"Ha! We got track and cars right here!" Joey said, exhaling. "And it's Sunday! Come on, one time for the big boys, Raceday Sunday, right here, right now. Me and you, like it used to be, no chicks, no break-ups, no heart aches. Hot Wheels versus Matchbox." Jimmy grinned at Joey.

"Alright, man, if it will help you clear your mind. But I'm going to smoke you; I hope you're ready for that disappointment, too." The boys lined their cars up side by side, and each one gunned his engine at the other.

"On the count of three!" Joey shouted at Jimmy. They started counting simultaneously, just like when they were six years old, and when they both reached three, they hit the gas. Tires squealed and engines sang and they both took off down the strip. Joey had pulled ahead, but Jimmy was gaining ground quickly. They were almost down the quarter-mile when Jimmy pulled even with Joey; they both looked over at each other and smiled. Joey smashed the gas all the way to the floor and pulled slightly ahead of Jimmy once more; he was a hood's length ahead when they crossed the finish line and his front side passenger tire passed over a sharp rock and blew out. Joey lost control instantly and his car went into a roll. The car flipped side over side a total of six times and came to rest on its tires, a mangled heap. Jimmy screeched to a halt and jumped out of his car. He ran to Joey's car and tried to pull the door open; it was stuck fast. He looked through the window and realized Joey wasn't in the car, at least not all of him, anyway. Lying in the passenger seat was Joey's right arm. Jimmy backed up, horrified, and looked around for the rest of Joey. He couldn't see anything in the dark, only the patch of the strip lit up by his headlights. He called out to Joey and got no response. Jimmy looked around more frantically and then finally heard a moan behind him, about twenty yards away. He moved towards the sound and then saw a human shaped lump in the darkness. Joey lay on the ground in a growing pool of blood and looked vacantly up at the stars. Jimmy knelt next to him and stroked his forehead.

"Hang in there buddy, gonna get you some help. Just stay with me."

"Nah, too late buddy," Joey coughed. "Guess that settles it though. Hot Wheels are the best." He exhaled one last time and died there on the side of the road.

Jimmy almost didn't go to the viewing; he didn't want to see his friend like that. He wanted to remember him alive and laughing, not dead and quiet forever. Joey's dad finally got through to him, though, and he agreed to go see his friend one last time. He put on the required black clothing, and brought something with him to place in the casket with Joey, mostly out of tradition. They drove to the funeral home. Jimmy waited for all of Joey's family to pay their respects and to be the last person to view him before they closed the casket. Jimmy walked up to the casket and leaned over the opening, peering in to Joey's forever still face.

"I miss you terribly already, buddy, hope the other side is treating you well," Jimmy said. Joey did not respond. "I brought you something to make the afterlife a little more pleasant, according to the Egyptians anyway." Jimmy reached in to his pocket and pulled out a quarter bag of weed. He looked back over both of his shoulders to make sure he was alone and then slipped the bag inside Joey's burial suit lapel, hidden and out of view. Jimmy patted Joey's chest where the bag was and looked at him one last time.

"See ya around, buddy," he said, and turned away from the casket.

Joey was buried the next afternoon during a rain storm. The rain was kind enough to wait until after the service was over and the mourners had left the graveside. As the workers were beginning to put the dirt in the hole, the skies opened up and a torrent was unleashed. The workers hastily filled in the hole and got out of the rain. Unbeknownst to them, and Joey's family, for that matter, was that the funeral director had cut corners on embalming and burial expenses by not embalming Joey's corpse for one, and by using a duplicate casket to the one that Joey's family had chosen, for two, that was constructed of second rate materials. This allowed dirt and rain to seep in to the casket and mingle with Joey's decomposing body. This wouldn't have made much of a difference underground, had Jimmy not introduced the foreign package to the casket and patted it before he left: doing so caused the bag of weed to split open inside of Joey's jacket and spill out. The seeds inside of the weed were eventually germinated by the potent mixture of dirt, rainwater, and decomposing Joey. The seedlings managed to sprout, and found their way out of the casket, stretching and reaching and growing towards the surface, until, months after Joey's burial, the sprouts broke the surface and soaked up some much needed sun that was shining on the graveyard.

A year to the day of Joey's death Jimmy made his way to the graveyard to say hi to his friend for the first time since his burial. Jimmy had wanted to make the journey many times before, but just couldn't bring himself to it, until the anniversary of the accident. Something clicked inside of him and he decided to just go. He parked his car and made his way to Joey's plot. He walked up on it, not noticing the plant at first. He just looked at Joey's headstone and kept reading the birth and death dates over and over again. Tears finally welled up in his eyes and as he was wiping them away he looked towards the ground and saw the plant growing out of Joey's burial plot. It was the prettiest marijuana plant that Jimmy had ever seen, it hadn't started to bud yet, but the leaves were full and green, and there wasn't a single insect anywhere near it. The dewdrops that were still on the leaves caught every beam of sunshine and cast it at Jimmy, making the plant seem to glow. Jimmy knelt down next to it and stroked a few of the leaves and decided right there to dig it up. He drove immediately to the local hardware store and purchased a garden spade and a medium sized clay plot to put the plant in. He raced back to the gravesite and set about removing the plant from the ground as gingerly as possible. He dug a pot sized hole around the plant and carefully extracted it from the ground; the plant came out fairly easily. He placed it in the pot he bought, and then laid down a bouquet of flowers he had purchased to cover the hole.

Jimmy took the plant home and set it on his back porch where it would catch good rays during the day, then in the heat of the afternoon would be in the shade. He decided to call the plant Joey, in honor of his friend, and would routinely talk to it like his friend was actually in the room. He had read somewhere that if you talked nicely to plants and played them soft music, they would respond and grow better. It was not because he was losing his mind. And it seemed to work: the plant stayed robust and grew and finally, after nurturing it for a month, it started to bud. Jimmy had never seen buds like this, not in all of his issues of High Times, or at the Hemp-Fests that he and Joey used to go to. The buds changed color depending on which angle you looked at them: sometimes they looked like red-hair, other times it was purple, still others it looked like they were frost-colored. When the buds looked big and healthy enough, Jimmy clipped them off and hung them to dry them out. Jimmy noticed that when he clipped the buds, a little spot of red sap would emerge from the cut and harden. He didn't pay much attention to this though, and when he finished, he had seven big buds hanging and drying in his closet. He removed them from the closet after a couple of days, and took one of the smaller of the buds to his rolling tray. He snapped off a piece of the bud and put it in a brand new grinder, he wanted to keep the keef from this bud separate. He ground it up and dumped it on his tray, there wasn't a single seed to be seen anywhere. And even though it was ground up, the weed still kept changing colors. Jimmy grabbed his King-Size Zig-Zags and rolled himself a moderate spliff from the pile of broken up weed. When he was satisfied that the paper was dry, he went out to the garage and sat in one of the two recliners that was out there. Between the two recliners was a TV tray with a couple of well-worn drink coasters and an even more well-worn ashtray. Behind the ashtray was a pair of computer speakers with an MP3 player plugged in to it. Jimmy switched on the speakers, and hit play on the MP3 player, "Illusion" by VNV Nation issued forth from the speakers. Jimmy saluted the empty recliner with the spliff and his lighter.

"Here's to you, Joey, best friend a guy could have and gone too soon." He punctuated his statement with a flick of the lighter and a puff on the spliff. He got the cherry going on the joint and took a deep drag, filling his lungs and holding it in. His lungs instantly felt like happiness, like a rainbow had exploded in there and gotten all over the rest of his innards. He held his breath still and felt his face turning red and hot and then when he could hold it no longer, exhaled a huge cloud. He hadn't turned on the vent fan in the garage, so the exhaled cloud just swirled in the middle of the garage. He looked at the spliff, and narrowed his eyes at it, like he was suspicious of it all of a sudden, but then brought it back to his mouth and took another large pull on it. He held this hit in as long as he could, like the first, and exhaled another large cloud that joined the first one in the center of the garage. The clouds swirled together into kind of a lazy weed tornado and Jimmy found himself staring into it. The smoke continued to swirl and billow, then it started to take a shape. A human shape. Jimmy's mouth dropped open as the smoke human began to form and gain a face. It was Joey, standing in the middle of the cloud, in the middle of the garage.

116

Jimmy realized he was standing up, and was almost face-to-face with Smoke Joey. Smoke Joey was smiling at him, but hadn't done anything yet except stand there. Jimmy felt weak in the legs and made a move to sit back in his recliner, but couldn't take his eyes off of Smoke Joey, so he ended up on his ass in the middle of the garage. Smoke Joey made a move to try to help Jimmy up, but his smoke hand went right through Jimmy's solid one.

"Whoops, guess that don't work," Joey said.

"Gog, buggle rump." Jimmy said. He still had the joint in his hand and looked back at it again, then back at Smoke Joey. "I'm sorry, what I meant to say was, 'What the actual fuck?'" Jimmy had scooted across the floor, back against the recliner.

"Well, buddy, there's no easy way to say this, so I'll just put it out there. You're smoking me."

"That sounds absurd and disgusting."

"Well, it's the truth. The plant you got from my grave was grown out of me with the help of Mother Nature and some shoddy funeral practices. And you leaving that weed in my coat, that was the main part, otherwise I'd just be a rich earth stew right now."

"So, the plant is you, I'm smoking you and breathing you, and now you're back and I don't think I can deal with this holyshitI'mfuckinghighwhatthefuck…." Jimmy started breathing heavier and more rapidly.

"Easy, killer, or you're going to hyperventilate," Smoke Joey said. "Get up in that chair and mellow out." Jimmy slid up into the chair, never taking his eyes off of Smoke Joey. Eventually his breathing returned to normal.

117

"So why are you here? Why are you back?"

"Because we're best buds, Jimmy, and its super boring on the other side. First off, there's no heaven or hell. Every person, when they die, releases an energy. It usually gets released when the body is embalmed, but my energy stayed with my body because I was part of a greedy scheme. This energy usually disperses after a while and is repurposed into a new energy that is used in a new life, that's where re-incarnation and past life memories come from. Some of the energies are stubborn and stick around for a while, attached to something or someone they held dear in their life, and that's where ghosts and poltergeists come from. But then there are some of us who are real stubborn, and we find a way back through another living thing, like mediums and psychics. I was able to find my way back through a weed plant."

"So the weed plant is a psychic," Jimmy dead-panned.

"NO, fool, it's just a living thing I came back through. Psychics and mediums are the best conduits to return through, but any living thing will do. Come on, how awesome is it that I am basically reincarnated as a weed plant, AND you get to still hang out with me. I thought you'd be thrilled."

"It's just...a lot...um...to absorb. At once. While high."

"I see your point. Sorry, it is earth-shattering, I agree."

"So are you here for good, or..."

"I'm here for good in the plant. I will always be around as long as the plant continues to live. In order to see me, however, you have to smoke me like you just did, and my energy can present itself in the smoke. Plus, it gets you really fucking high, so there's that." Smoke Joey smiled down at Jimmy and Jimmy could see that he was
118

starting to dissipate. It would have been much worse had he turned the vent fan on, Jimmy thought, Joey might not have even gotten the chance to show himself.

"It's good to see you, Joey, even if it is right through you."

"It's good to see you, too, Jimmy. Now fire that joint back up and let's hang out for a while."

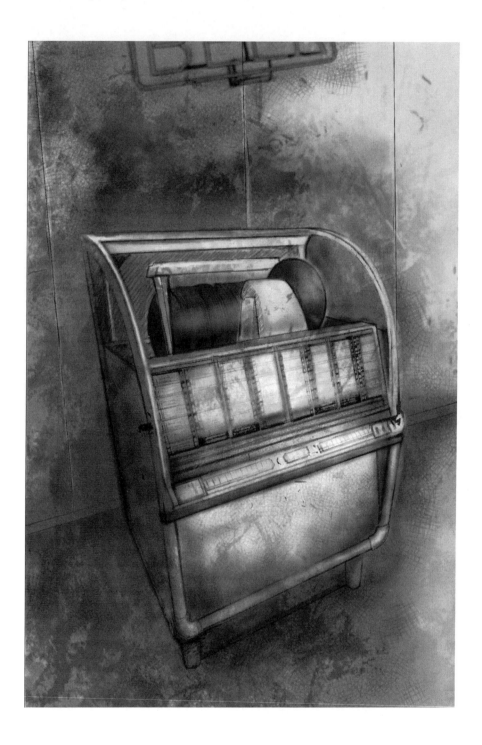

The Midnight Nomads

Happy Hour was waning at Tookie's Somewhere Else, which was actually only an hour, from 8 to 9 o' clock P.M. Tookie's was a dingy little bar that had two beers on tap and neither was very cold. Luckily, the freezer worked fine, so the ice-cold mugs the draft beer was poured in would compensate. The jukebox, installed decades previous and still with the 45's it originally came with, was warbling out Patsy Cline's "Stop the World (And Let Me Off)". The many years of cigarette smoke had left a permanent haze to the bar, to the effect that even if no one was smoking, there was still a London fog inside. The two pool tables that stood off to the side of the warped bar were in just as bad a shape as the rest of the place: one was unplayable from ripped felt, the other stopped accepting quarters a decade ago, so it was used on the honor system: free play as long as you kept drinking. There were pool sticks hung on the wall, but none of those were usable either, you had to bring your own stick to play. No one was playing pool this evening, there were only three people in the bar: Holly, the 28 year old bartender, Tookie, Holly's grandfather and proprietor of the saloon, as well as Lew Jackson, local meth dealer. The bar itself was situated along a dusty road that led out of town, "Last Chance to Wet Your Whistle for 100 miles…Come on in!!" a sign proclaimed outside. These days, few people wet their whistles at Tookie's, however, and the lack of income had begun to show in the upkeep of the bar. The reason the people stayed away wasn't the not-so-cold draft beer, or the ripped pool table, but Lew Jackson. The only reason you went to Tookie's these days was if you were from out of town or looking for a fix. The bar was more meth lab than ale house and all the locals knew that. The county sheriff was too busy with the border patrol, so it left a perfect opportunity for Lew Jackson to set up shop. He strong armed Tookie into putting a shed out back to do the cooking and put his chemist in there, and then made an office of the bar from which to conduct business. Tookie was too old to put up any sort of a fight, and Holly didn't want her old man harmed, so she kept silent. Jackson made sure the place stayed open as business began to decline: he would pay the rent and bills, and Tookie would be indebted to him and forced to let him keep plying his drugs.

The record on the jukebox switched to The Statler Brothers' "Bed of Rose's" and the three sat there in silence: Holly cleaning mugs, Tookie reading a newspaper, Jackson in the corner by the broken pool table, scrolling through an address book with a rotary phone on the table next to him.

"Fuckin' recession," Jackson muttered to himself. "Gotta find some new damn customers." Tookie glanced over the top of his newspaper at Jackson and shook his head; Jackson didn't notice. Holly just clenched her teeth and kept wiping mugs she had already cleaned three times. Then, from outside the bar, came the sound of running motors, loud, and lots of them. Tookie recognized them immediately for what they were: motorcycles. Tookie couldn't tell how many there were, but he figured it had to be a dozen or more, the din they were creating. Jackson looked up from his address book, listening to the cacophony of motors.

"Look alive, beer wench," Lew said to Holly, "sounds like you got some customers."

"How do you know they're not your customers?" Holly spat back. Lew just looked at her and gave her the finger. After a few seconds all of the motors died out and things were silent. Then the front door banged open and there stood "The biggest sumbitch I ever seen", was how Holly would later describe it. Standing about 6'8" and almost as wide, the man had to duck to enter the doorway. He came through the threshold and stopped, looking around. He was dressed in faded, dusty black jeans that ended in huge, leather boots with silver spurs on the back that jingled when he took a step. His top half was clad in a leather vest that looked like it was made from five cows, worn over a shirt that had The Rolling Stones "Lips" logo on it. Three heavy metal chains hung from his belt and stretched to his back pocket to a leather billfold that was sticking out. He had a beard that stretched to the middle of his chest, but was separated into two braids on either side of his mouth. He wore a pair of mirrored aviator sunglasses, even though it was pitch black outside and he had a black bandana tied around his head. There were patches on the front of his vest in black and white embroidery with red stitching that proclaimed him a member of something called "The Midnight Nomads" and that he was "Sgt. at Arms" and that his name was "Viking". He surveyed the room for a few moments, then ducked and went back out the door the way he came. The three remaining occupants of Tookie's Somewhere Else just looked at each other. The 45 on the jukebox was now Juice Newton's "Queen of Hearts".

The front door had remained open after the giant had retreated through it, and now there were audible footsteps approaching the front door, it sounded like an army. The footsteps got closer until another form filled the doorframe, this one not nearly as big as the previous occupant, and female. She was stunning, and even old Tookie felt a little tickle in his crotch, something that hadn't worked in ten years. She was about 5' 7", slender and top heavy. She wore jeans similar to the one called Viking, but more form fitting, as if they'd been painted on. Her boots were more feminine, ending in three inch steel spikes at the heel. She was wearing a leather vest that had similar patches to the one Viking was wearing, only hers said "President" and the name she bore was "Stabitha". She also wore the same style of sunglasses as Viking, though hers were obviously a lot smaller. She had a large mane of curly, black hair that was held back under a black silk scarf tied around her head. She stopped just inside the door as Viking had done, removed her sunglasses and looked at the three occupants. She smiled and entered the room fully, striding to the bar where Holly had absentmindedly stopped wiping the glass in her hand and just stood there, towel in one hand, glass in the other. After Stabitha had entered and crossed the room, more figures followed behind her, Viking was one of them. The rest of the group was of varying sizes, although none as big as Viking, and there were 10 of them in all, including Viking and Stabitha. Standing at Stabitha's right side was a thin man of about 6', with a close cropped black goatee and identical outfit to Viking's, except his shirt advertised the band Motörhead and he was bald headed. The patches on his kutte proclaimed him "Vice President" and his moniker was "Gypsy". Viking stood behind Stabitha and Gypsy at the bar; the rest of the group stood just inside the doorway. Lew Jackson kept his seat in the dark corner across the room, put away his address book, and sized up the group of bikers. One of them had his back to Jackson; on the back of his cut was a picture of a skeleton riding a skeletal horse that was reared back on its hind legs. "The Midnight Nomads" was written above the skeletal logo, and underneath "Est. '66" was written. While Jackson was looking over the bikers, another turned his back to Jackson, and although the logo and name were the same, underneath it said "Prospect". Stabitha spoke to Holly, in a voice that had a slight accent to it, but Holly couldn't place it, nor could Tookie or Jackson, for that matter.

"Good evening, gracious hosts. My traveling companions are quite thirsty and weary. How much to keep us in drink all night?" she inquired Holly.

"Um, well, you can start a tab and I can add it all up at the end of the night, that's how we usually do it…" Holly had started to explain to the woman, when Jackson interrupted.

"Well, little lady," he said, addressing Stabitha, "ya'll give me a thousand dollars and you can drink what you want, hell, you can even take a pool table with you."

"I assure you, that won't be necessary," she said sweetly to Jackson. She snapped her fingers at one of her posse. A burly man with a sizeable beer gut strode forward, carrying a black, leather briefcase, attached to his wrist with a long silver chain. His manner of dress was similar to the others, his shirt advertised "The Grateful Dead" and his patches proclaimed him as "Treasurer" and that his name was "Buddha". He set the briefcase on the warped wood of the bar and opened it. From it he withdrew ten crisp hundred dollar bills and laid them on the bar in front of Holly. At the sight of the money, Jackson was across the room and behind the bar in a flash. He got behind the bar in enough time to see the briefcase before Buddha closed it; it was stock full of cash of all denominations, and from different countries. Jackson figured there could easily have been a million dollars in that case. His brain starting turning gears on how he was going to get his hands on it. Jackson made to grab at the money on the bar; Stabitha put her forefinger on the bills before he could snatch them up and held them in place.

"This will cover our expenses here this evening, and not a penny more."

"Certainly," Jackson said with a sly grin. "Drink away! Play some pool! Get nice and fucked up!" Stabitha removed her finger from the cash and Jackson was able to put it in his pocket. She motioned to the rest of the group to join her at the bar, and then turned to Holly.

"Ten of your finest beers, if you please," she said with a sweet smile.

"Draft or bottle? May I suggest bottle, as the draft is lukewarm when it leaves the tap and don't get much colder after that."

"I'm sure Buddha won't mind the temperature of anything you serve him, but the rest of us will go with bottle please." Holly looked at Buddha and asked which he preferred.

"Both." Holly placed ten bottled beers on the bar and drew one from the draft and set that down next to the others. Buddha grabbed both of his and drank two-fisted. The rest of the group grabbed their beers nonchalantly and retreated to the tables opposite the pool tables. Viking grabbed his bottle, and rather than twisting off the cap of the bottle, he flicked it off with a swift movement of his thumb. He then drained the beer in one swallow, setting the bottle back on the bar.

"Another," he said, and when he received that one, repeated the procedure.

"Slow down, big fella," Stabitha purred.

"Yes, ma'am," Viking said, and nursed his third beer. Gypsy had walked over to the jukebox and was perusing the selection. "In Dreams" by Roy Orbison was in current rotation; Gypsy reached down and unplugged the machine.

"Hey, I like Orbison!" Tookie protested. Gypsy regarded him with a look, Stabitha told him to plug it back in. He obliged.

"I prefer Johnny Cash," he said with a smile. "You don't have any on this machine."

"Sorry, fella, had one in there, but it got scratched mighty fierce one time, had to take it out."

"No worries, old timer," Gypsy said with the same smile, and turned back to his beer.

By this time, Lew Jackson had slunk back to his dark corner of the room, and sat in the chair next to the table with the phone on it. He took out his address book, and leafed through it. He was going to need some of the toughest S.O.B.'s he knew if he was going to get that briefcase.

"Gonna need at least three guys to take down that big mother fucker," he thought to himself. "They don't look like they have any weapons, if I get enough guns here, I can make this quick." He picked six names out of his book, and took a look at the bikers one more time. The pile of bottles had grown, thanks mostly to the drinking habits of Viking and Buddha, but to Jackson, the rest of the gang wasn't getting liquored up fast enough. He was going to have to get these guys shit-faced if his guys were going to even have a chance at getting that money.

"Hey, guys, let's make this a real party!" Jackson crowed. "I got a bottle of 50 year old single malt that has been waiting for the right moment. I think this is that moment." Jackson went behind the bar and reached below it, extracting the bottle in question. He had Holly line up twelve shot glasses (none for Tookie, he'd been sober six years and counting) and poured the shots. Holly delivered them to each of the men and Stabitha. Jackson raised a toast to the room and everyone drank, except Holly, who faked hers and poured it out when no one was looking. Jackson took the rest of the bottle and set it on one of the tables, proclaiming it bought and paid for by the group. Buddha grabbed the bottle and took a mighty swig from it. Jackson retreated back to his corner and dug out his address book again. He kept his eyes on the bikers as he dialed each number, and spoke in hushed tones so that none of the group could hear what he had to say. He dialed each of his confederates and told them the plan, choosing to leave out how much money was actually at stake. He would compensate his crew, but not as richly as he would compensate himself.

For the next half hour, Jackson watched the bikers drink, talk, smoke and laugh, seemingly getting more inebriated as the minutes clicked away. Midnight rolled around and Jackson could hear vehicles approaching. It was almost go-time. Jackson excused himself from the room and went outside. He'd told his guys to gather by the meth shed, they could make a noiseless entry from that direction and be able to catch the bikers off guard. All six of his guys had guns of various sizes, ranging from pistols to shotguns; one guy had a semi-automatic rifle. He told the group that the first one to take down was the big guy, you couldn't miss him. After that they would hold the room hostage until they got the money case, then they would execute every last one of those dirty bikers and scavenge them for other goodies, maybe even find a way to sell off their bikes and make even more cash. The greed between the men was contagious and overwhelming; they couldn't wait to pull this off. Jackson signaled to his men to get in position, three would go through the back door, while Jackson and the other three went in the front, ensuring that none of the bikers escaped.

As planned, the four men ran in the front door, and seconds later the other three came charging in the back. The men leveled their weapons at the bikers and told them to put their hands up. The bikers looked at their muggers and did nothing.

"I SAID HANDS FUCKING UP," Lew Jackson screamed!! Stabitha made no move to comply, nor did her gang. The only one who moved was Viking, who took a few steps towards Jackson and his men.

"FREEZE, UGLY!!" Jackson said, as someone behind him muttered, "Holy shit, look at that fucking guy." Viking did not freeze and took another step towards Jackson. The man to the right of Jackson raised his shotgun and fired pointblank into Viking's chest, knocking

129

him back a few feet into the jukebox and obliterating the lips on his t-shirt, along with most of the skin and muscle underneath it. Viking went down on his large posterior with a grunt and did not get up, Holly screamed at the sight of a man with his chest blown away and then fainted behind the bar. Tookie stood up from his chair, shouting "No!" at what he had just seen. The bikers still had not raised their hands. Jackson pointed his gun at the one they called Buddha and demanded he bring forth the case. Buddha did not move, except to bring the beer back to his lips. Jackson, by now furious, shot the beer out of Buddha's hand.

"Bad move, dude," one of the bikers said. Buddha brushed the broken glass from the shattered bottle out of his beard, and then proceeded to raise the mug of beer that was in his other hand. Jackson shot that one, too. A low whistle came from another one of the bikers. Buddha now turned his gaze to Jackson and stared at him with cold eyes.

"I was drinking that," he said. Something exploded in Jackson's mind at this statement and all he saw was red. He proceeded to empty the gun into Buddha's face. He fell from the chair he sat in and landed facedown. Jackson dropped his now empty gun and grabbed the shotgun that had been used to fell Viking. He waved the gun at the rest of the bikers.

"Somebody bring me that fucking briefcase right now, or I'll slaughter the rest of you fucks." Gypsy finally made a move towards the fallen Buddha and picked the briefcase up off the ground. Jackson turned the shotgun on him.

"Alright, bring it here, Skinny," Jackson commanded. Gypsy took a set of keys from Buddha's pocket and unlocked the case from his unmoving wrist. He stood up and walked slowly over to Jackson and his three men, but did not hold the case out for him to grab. Instead, he just looked at Jackson and smiled.

"What's so funny, Fancy Pants? Got a joke you wanna tell the rest of the room?" Jackson demanded.

"Nope, nothing funny at all," Gypsy said, and as he finished his statement a loud growling began somewhere inside the room.

"What the fuck is that?" Jackson exclaimed, looking around wildly.

"Your reckoning," Gypsy said and swung the briefcase in an upward arc that connected with the chin of the guy Jackson had gotten the shotgun from. The force of the swing knocked the man's head clean off, and his headless body stood stock-still for a moment before crumpling to the floor and gushing blood out of the neck hole. His head rolled across the floor and came to rest at the feet of one of the pool tables. The growling continued to grow louder as all of this happened and erupted into a roar. Suddenly, Viking was on his feet and across the room, directly in front of Jackson and the two remaining men at his side. His shirt was a ragged mess where he had been shot, but his chest showed no hint of wounds. He reached over and palmed both men's heads, squeezing tightly at the temples. Jackson's jaw had gone slack, the shotgun forgotten. Somewhere in the back of his mind, he could hear the other three men at the back of the room screaming and firing shots from their guns that were having no effect on their targets. Viking took the two men he had a grasp of and with amazing force, smashed their heads together in a meaty, bloody explosion, silencing their screams forever. Stabitha watched with a smirk as her gang descended on the three remaining men, their fangs bared, and their vampire bloodlust about to be satiated. Buddha had gathered himself off the floor and was taking another large swig out of the single malt. He swallowed and grimaced; he coughed and spat out a bullet. He walked across the room to where Gypsy was still standing with the bloody briefcase. Gypsy handed it back to him and Buddha reattached the chain to his wrist.

"You're going to clean this, right?" Buddha asked. Gypsy flashed him a smile.

"Of course, brother, you shouldn't even need to ask." Gypsy picked up the briefcase and licked some of the blood off.

"Not with your tongue, bro," Buddha laughed. "Prospect!!" The biker with the word "prospect" stitched under his logo came forward. He didn't have his fangs bared like all the rest, because he didn't have any yet.

"Yes, sir!" he said eagerly.

"You get to earn your patch tonight," Buddha said. "Grab Slack-Jaw over there and sit him in this chair." Prospect grabbed Jackson and guided him to the chair after relieving him of the shotgun. Jackson sat in absolute shock, his mind had checked out on him. Stabitha approached Jackson and put her spike-heeled foot against his shoulder. She pushed hard enough to break the skin and puncture, the pain was enough to bring Jackson back to a certain level of clarity.

"AHHHHHHHHH!!!" he screamed. Stabitha smiled down at him and removed her foot, then grabbed his chin with a firm strong hand.

"It's not nice to steal from people, Mr. Jackson. You've had to learn that the hard way, and it's a lesson you'll be taking to your grave." She squeezed his jaw and the bones snapped effortlessly in her fingers. Jackson screamed again, garbled this time by broken bones

132

and a swelling face. Stabitha looked at Prospect and called him forth.

"Are you ready to earn your patch and join The Midnight Nomads, Prospect?" she asked. He nodded eagerly and she had him kneel in front of the mewling Lew Jackson. She took a finger and slit her own wrist, pressing the wound to Prospect's mouth. He suckled at her wrist for a few minutes until she withdrew her arm and let the wound heal itself instantly. Prospect knelt where he was, trembling, with his eyes closed. He suddenly threw his head back and his mouth and eyes flew open. His eyes were pure white for a few seconds, and then the color came back to the irises, a deep red. Fangs descended from his upper jaw, knocking out the human canines that had once been housed there. Prospect's trembling subsided and he lowered his head; he was now looking in to the ruined face of Lew Jackson. Full and complete terror now engulfed Jackson, his bladder let loose and he wet his pants.

"Aww, look, he went and marinated himself," Prospect wisecracked. The rest of the vampire biker gang howled with laughter. Except for Viking, he just smiled. Prospect opened his mouth and stretched his jaw, really feeling his fangs. Then he pounced on Lew Jackson and bit his throat out, taking in his first meal as a full-fledged member of the gang. The rest of the bikers hooted and cheered, and when he was done and Lew Jackson was drained of all of his blood, Prospect stood and was surrounded by his new brothers. They clapped him on the back and shoulders and ruffled his scruffy hair, and then they had him remove the vest he was wearing. Stabitha came forth with a new kutte for him to don, only there was no name stitched to this one, and where his old kutte had once said "Prospect" his new one said "Est. '14".

"As we welcome our new brother," she said proudly, "we await his choice in name. Dear Brother, to what should we refer to you as?"

"I was almost used to being called 'Prospect'", he said with a chuckle, wiping some blood from the corner of his mouth. "I think I like the name 'Gremlin'."

"Then Gremlin you shall be," Stabitha said. "Welcome, Gremlin. Nomads, welcome Brother Gremlin!" A chorus of cheers rose, and the bikers started to chant his name in unison. After a few minutes, Stabitha quieted them.

"The celebration will continue, as I believe we have paid for a night of drinking, but first we have other business to attend." Her gaze shifted to the bar, where Tookie was now trying to roust his fainted granddaughter. In one swift move, she jumped and twisted in midair, landing in a crouched position atop the bar and looking down at the last two living occupants of Tookie's Somewhere Else.

"Please," Tookie said, looking up at Stabitha, "please don't kill us. We won't say nothing, promise. You guys just have your fun and mosey on and I'll pretend like nothing happened here." He coughed into his forearm when he was finished talking, and spit a wad of phlegm on to the floor.

"We're not going to hurt you or your precious granddaughter, not tonight, or ever," Stabitha said. "We initially came here to offer you an opportunity; we weren't expecting your business partner to be here."

"Oh, he's no partner of mine," Tookie interrupted. "He just barged in here one day and took over my bar, ran off all my regulars, starting slinging dope. I just couldn't fight him." Tookie was looking down at his granddaughter again, she was still passed out. "You said you came here to offer me something, what is it?" Stabitha looked down at the old man and smiled.

"Someone would like to say hello." She looked back over her shoulder and nodded. Tookie could hear footsteps approaching, but did not stand. A face appeared next to Stabitha, leaning over the bar and looking down at Tookie.

"Hello, Tookie, been a long time." If Lew Jackson had still been alive, he'd have recognized this guy as the one who had been wearing the patch that said "Est. '76". Tookie hadn't recognized him as he came in, because he could barely see past the end of his nose without his glasses, and only marginally better when he had them on. Now that the face was up close enough for Tookie to see it, he broke out in to a wide grin.

"Smoak! Phil Smoak! Jesus, it's been…Damn, it's good to see you!" Tookie was looking into the face of his old army buddy; they had fought Charlie together at Dong Ha Province, and both made it out alive, with Tookie carrying Smoak five miles on his back when Smoak had taken a bullet. They had come home after the war and stayed in touch for a few years before Tookie lost touch with his buddy. Tookie now looked at Smoak in wonder, marveling at how young he looked.

"Geez, Smoak, you haven't aged a day since the 'Nam." Phil Smoak looked back at his friend with a smile.

"It's Smokey now," he said, tapping the patch on his vest. "I'll cut to the chase, Tookie; I want you to come with us. I can already see you don't have much time left." As if to emphasize this, Tookie coughed hard and spat again.

135

"What about Holly? I can't leave her here, I'm all she's got," Tookie pleaded.

"If you join us, she has us as well. We will fund this bar and get it back to being a good place again, and we can use it as a home base whenever we're in the area. You don't have to leave her forever." Holly had started to stir on the floor behind the bar; Tookie helped her to sit up. She opened her eyes and saw Stabitha perched on the bar and Smokey leaning over it. She gasped and tried to retreat but Tookie grabbed her and told her it was all right.

"They're friends," he said, "believe it or not. They've taken care of our problem and have offered me a solution to mine." She looked him in the eyes and knew he was telling the truth. Her Grandpa had never looked her in the eye and lied to her. He turned to Stabitha and addressed her.

"I'll go, but I think I'm going to need some time to get used to this blood and death thing. That shit was crazy." Smokey came around the bar and offered a hand to both Tookie and his granddaughter to help them up.

"It does take some time, friend, but it's no worse than the 'Nam. And we only take those that deserve it, like Mr. Jackson and his cohorts over there. As a Prospect, you're our eyes and ears during the day when we can't go out. You find the ones who deserve to be ended, and we take care of it." They had come from around the back of the bar, and were now in the presence of the rest of the group. Stabitha dismounted the bar and approached Tookie. She held out the kutte previously worn by Gremlin.

"Here, Prospect. Put this on." Tookie slipped his arms in and pulled it on. It fit perfectly and felt good on his body. He looked around at the faces of the bikers; it was hard to believe that all of these kind faces were tearing people apart only minutes previous. Suddenly, Viking stepped forward, ragged shirt and all. He put a giant hand on Tookie's shoulder and gave it a light squeeze.

"Prospect," Viking said, and smiled.

Nights in Shining Armor

Kenny Bartlett opened his eyes and found they were the only thing that could move. He shifted his eyes wildly from side to side, fear growing rapidly in his mind.

"Ah, I see we are awake," came a voice from across the room. Kenny heard footsteps approaching, and then a face filled his vision. One he recognized from somewhere, but was unable to place where exactly. Kenny tried to say something, but his vocal cords, like the rest of his body, were not working.

"Welcome back to the world of the waking, Mr. Bartlett. We are going to discuss several things here today, although the conversation may be a bit one sided, in my favor." The man chuckled at this last statement and proceeded to look Kenny over. Kenny was sure he knew this guy from somewhere, but the terror he was experiencing from being a captive and the compounded fear of not being able to move a single limb of his body was making it difficult to think and place faces and names. The man spoke to him again.

"Firstly, Mr. Bartlett, let me describe what is happening to you right now. I've introduced suxamethonium chloride to your system, also known as Succinylcholine. It is a paralytic agent that allows you to see and hear and feel everything going on around you, but there is nothing you can do about it. When used in large doses it is extremely fatal, but you're not here to die so I'm using a controlled IV drip to let enough into your system to keep you in this condition. You may be asking yourself why I'm doing this, and we'll get to that eventually, but here's some more of what's going on." The man brought the IV drip into Kenny's field of vision and tapped the plastic bag.

"In here, there are also nutrients and vitamins that are going to keep you alive. I said that you are not here to die, but rest assured, you are going to wish you were. I have also installed a colostomy bag for waste removal, can't having you stewing in your own urine and fecal matter where you're going." Kenny tried his hardest to move a limb: a toe, a finger, anything. He tried to yell, to scream at the top of his lungs, but his mouth would not open and no sound would issue forth. All he could do was shift his eyes about wildly. The man noticed him doing this and laughed.

"Ha-ha! Yes, keep trying! That's the fighting spirit! That spirit will keep you going for the next few months, I think, but it, too, will be broken, just like you. You worthless, thieving son of a bitch." The last line the man spoke was delivered with absolute coldness and hate. This guy really had it in for Kenny. He walked over to Kenny and moved his head so he was looking to his left. He could now see the IV drip and where it was connected in the crook of his arm. Beyond that he could see a wall with stairs leading up it. On the wall were several photos of Kenny, going about his various daily activities. This guy had been following Kenny and spying on him for a while it seemed, and Kenny had no idea. He started to surmise that he was in a basement of some sort. He could see where the wall with the stairs connected with another wall and the dirt floor that was underneath them. In the corner where the walls joined, was a full sized suit of medieval knight's armor, extremely shiny from polishing.

"You know, at first I didn't think I would be able to pull this off; that maybe I lacked the courage and the conviction. But after watching you day after day and taking stock of everything that you do, I found the courage and the conviction and the strength to do what must be done." The man repositioned Kenny's head so he was looking straight up again. He leaned over Kenny and looked into his eyes.

"You could have avoided all of this if you weren't such a thieving bastard. Or maybe if someone had taught you your lesson earlier on, I wouldn't have to be doing this, but here we are, and it's too late for you to learn anything. Now you must be punished." Kenny's thoughts were still wildly racing, trying to put together who this guy was and what beef he had with him. He was still coming up empty, but the man kept calling him a thief, so that had to be a clue of some sort. He didn't think of himself as a thief, of course, he wasn't aware that he had stolen anything from anyone. He led a pretty simple life: he worked at the auto salvage yard just outside of town, he had a couple of drinking buddies he would meet up with most days after work, and there was his old lady that he came home to. They weren't married, but had been together since senior year in high school. He had been a jock with the football team and she had been a science nerd. He needed tutoring help to pass science and stay on the team, so he enlisted her assistance to garner a good enough grade. He became attracted to her after a few tutoring sessions when he noticed that under the bookishness and nerdy outer layer that there was a pretty hot chick in there. She was swept away by the fact that a jock would be interested in her, so she fell for him pretty quickly. Kenny was a decent football player, but not good enough for the colleges to come calling with scholarships, so after graduation, they moved in together and he got a job at the salvage yard. They had been living together for about five years now, but the last three having been not all that happy for her. As Kenny went through his daily life, he began to get depressed on how his life was turning out, and thusly fell into the bottle more often. Most times he would just stumble through the door and pass out, but every so often he would come home coherent enough that arguments would ensue between him and her about his drinking and spending habits. These arguments would end violently, with him smacking her around a bit and telling her to shut up and don't worry about what he did. Over the past few months these arguments were happening more frequently, but still she stayed, hoping that one day he'd come out of it and come to his senses and be the guy she fell in love with. She didn't know that that was never going to happen.

The man had walked away from Kenny and he heard him flip a switch. Music issued forth from speakers around the room. It was "Everybody Hurts" from R.E.M. The man was humming along to the tune. He returned to Kenny and spoke to him again.

"Now, here's the next part of the plan. That suit of armor you saw in the corner? That's going to be your new home. Some of the things you've done should have put you in prison, but she's too much of a sweetheart to put you there, isn't she? Oh yeah, I know all about your proclivity to turn your girlfriend into a punching bag when you don't like what she's telling you. Saw all of that, too." He turned Kenny's head to the right and now he was looking at a different wall, but it also had pictures on it; these were of Kenny's girlfriend, but Kenny was nowhere in these photos, so this guy had been following her separately from him. "So, not only are you a thief, but a woman beater as well."

The song on the stereo changed to "Little Lies" by Fleetwood Mac. The man walked over to the suit of armor and brought it close to the table Kenny was on.

"Now, I have this suit of armor rigged to keep delivering the necessary fluids to your body to keep you alive and paralyzed. But that's not even the best part of the plan. I'm going to save that for later." The man disconnected the IV from the drip bag and connected it to a tube coming from the suit of armor. He then set about placing Kenny in the suit, one piece at a time until it was all assembled and Kenny was locked inside. The man stood the suit of armor up on its feet; Kenny was now upright and looking forward at yet another wall with pictures on it. These pictures were of the man and Kenny's girlfriend, only some of them were obviously taken when the two were much younger; they could have been as young as three years old in one picture. All the pictures of the two were of them smiling and laughing and taken by a third party. It was clear to Kenny now that this guy and his girlfriend knew each other, and for a long time.

"Alright, big guy, time to get you upstairs!" the man said. He strapped the suit of armor containing Kenny to a two-wheeled dolly and positioned him at the bottom of the stairs. "Now, I'm not a big beefy jock like you, so let's both hope I can get you up there without dropping you. I'd hate to kill you on accident, especially with my plan unfinished." The man grunted and pulled and, with a little struggle, managed to get Kenny all the way up the stairs. He opened the door at the top of the stairs and wheeled him out of the basement. They were now in what looked to be a large living room with all kinds of medieval artifacts all around the room. There was a blank corner, however, with a light shining on nothing; Kenny realized that this is where he was going to wind up. Sure enough, the man wheeled him over to the corner and unstrapped him from the dolly. He moved the dolly out of the way and rocked Kenny back and forth into position in the corner. The man came around to the front of the suit of armor and peered into the helmet into Kenny's face.

"OK, good. Can't see you from the outside. Can't hear you breathing in there, either. I can monitor your vitals on my cell phone with a sensor I installed in the armor; to make sure you stay alive. I want you alive for this, to see everything, and to bear witness to what I am about to do. See, I've had you here long enough that you're considered a missing person. Funny thing, though, is that Abigail didn't file it. Your boss did. Maybe she was happy to see you go, who knows? Tell you what, we'll both find out together when I have her over for dinner tonight." Kenny watched as the man pulled a cell phone out of his pocket and dialed a number. After a couple of seconds, he started to speak with someone.

"Abby, hi! It's George. Yes, I'm back in town, probably for good now. What are you doing this evening? Nothing? Would you like to come over to my new place and have dinner, just the two of us?" The man winked at Kenny in the suit and shot him a sly smile. "You would? Perfect! I'll pick you up around 7:30, how's that? Excellent, I'll see you then." George hung up the phone, and Kenny's mind started racing again. He now had a name to put to a face he was still trying to recognize. He'd only known one George in his life, and that had been in school. Then it hit him. George Dumas. A kid he'd picked on in middle school and high school until sophomore year when the kid had moved away. But why was he calling Kenny a thief? That part still didn't seem to fit. George walked back over to the armor and spoke to Kenny inside.

"It appears I have a date this evening. A friend and I have a lot of catching up to do. First, I have to clean up downstairs however; don't need her stumbling into that and discovering my little revenge scheme here." He smiled at Kenny again and then walked away. Kenny could hear him descending the stairs to the basement and then the music was turned up. The song now playing was "Standing Outside a Broken Phone Booth with Money in My Hand" by Primitive Radio Gods. Kenny shut his eyes and tried to think of a way out of this. He tried moving his mouth again, to no avail, as was the same with the rest of his body. Despair began to set in heavily. After a while, George came back upstairs and addressed Kenny once more.

"Alright, that's done. Guess I'll get myself cleaned up and get to the store to pick up dinner. I'm thinking shrimp Alfredo on fettuccini with garlic bread. It's her favorite, you know. Or maybe you don't. I don't think you spent much time learning what she did and didn't like, just wanted to slip her the old pickle and get your rocks off, right? Didn't have time to learn that lavender was her favorite scent, or that the koala was her favorite animal. That she loved

145

vampire stories but hated that 'Twilight' crap, or that she loved rainy days right after the rain stopped and all you could smell was nature. Nah, you were too involved in what you wanted and needed. And that's the difference between you and me: I love her and you love you." George turned and walked to the front door. He opened it and turned back once more to Kenny.

"See you in a little while!" he said, and then went out the door. Kenny heard the key turn in a lock and then all was silent. All he heard was his own thoughts.

Around 8:00 that night George returned with Abigail. Kenny saw them enter the front door and immediately he tried to cry out to her and flail any part of his body he could. Nothing happened; the drug in his system had rendered everything useless. George took Abby to the dining room and sat her at the table then went to the kitchen. Kenny could hear pots and pans clattering around as George cooked. George brought out a glass of wine for Abby as she waited. Kenny thought the food smelled amazing, and then wondered if he was ever going to taste anything like it ever again. George brought out two plates of food and his own wine glass with the rest of the bottle. They ate in relative silence, with Abby only commenting on the food and how good it was.

When they were finished eating, George directed Abby to the couch and sat her down; it was positioned across the room, opposite the suit of armor. He took the spot next to her on the couch. She was looking around and admiring all of the artifacts when her eyes finally settled on the suit of armor.

"Oh, that's a beautiful piece, George, is it a replica or an original?" she asked.

"Eh, it's just something I picked up recently. I believe it's real; the auction house had all the right papers, so I think its authentic 14th century. Real or not, though, I knew I had to have it, I knew you'd like it."

"Like it? I LOVE it; you know me and medieval stuff…"

"Yeah, like when we first read about King Arthur and the Knights of the Round Table in school. You were hooked immediately."

"You remember all the little things, don't you, George? I've always admired that about you. So what have you been doing for the past few years? It would seem as though you came in to a great amount of money, to be able to afford this house and everything in it, not to mention an authentic 14th century suit of armor. What has George Dumas been doing, besides obviously working out and tanning?" she asked with a smile.

"Well, as you know, I left sophomore year very abruptly."

"Yeah, you never even said goodbye. I was very hurt by that. I wasn't sure I was ever going to forgive you, but then I heard your voice this afternoon and all those bad feelings went away."

"Well, thank you for being so forgiving. When I tell you why I left I'm sure you'll understand. You see, I was being tormented by this guy in school; it started in middle school and continued until I left. I was almost to the point of doing something, like fighting back, or worse. But I told my folks about it and when they couldn't get any assistance from the school in the matter, they decided we would move away to complete my schooling. Doing so allowed me to finish early and then go to medical school. I threw myself into my schooling and managed to graduate early there, too. I went overseas for a little while and helped to work on a new cancer drug

147

that made me a lot of money. I decided to then come home and set up practice here, and reconnect with my best friend. You see, you're the only thing I regret leaving behind. I've thought about you every day I was gone. I guess what I mean to say is I came home for you, because I missed you, and I love you." By this time George had taken Abby's hand in his and was looking directly in her eyes. She returned his gaze and then she dropped her eyes to her lap.

"I love you, too, George. I'm sure that we should have been together in the past, and maybe we can in the future, but there's a slight problem. I'm currently in a relationship and have been with the same person since senior year of high school. It started out great, but the last few years have been awful. He drinks too much, gets abusive when he does and I'm pretty sure there have been other women."

"Sounds like a charmer," George said dryly. "What's his name, how did you guys meet?"

"Kenny Bartlett. He was a jock on the football team that needed my help to stay there. After you left, I didn't have any one to hang out with, really. So I started tutoring kids, hoping maybe I could make some friends that way. I did, too, but I also met Kenny that way. He took an interest in me outside of the books, and I hadn't been close to anything like that since you had gone. I fell for him and that was that. We graduated and I was going to go off to school, but my momma got sick and I had to stay close instead. Kenny and I moved into her house, he got a job at the salvage yard and things have gone downhill ever since." There were tears in Abby's eyes now, and they were starting to roll down her cheeks. George raised a tender hand and wiped them with a gentle thumb. She sniffled, and then looked at George. She smiled a little and he smiled back at her.

"We don't have to talk about this, if you don't want to," George said. "I don't want you to be upset. Let's talk about some of the good old days."

"It's okay, George," Abby said. "It helps to talk about it, to not keep it in. The only person I can talk to right now is Momma, and she doesn't talk back." She gave a little chuckle, followed by another sniffle. George brought her in close for an embrace, and Abby didn't resist. He held her like that for a few minutes and she cried a little more. Finally she pulled back and chuckled again, wiping her eyes with the back of her hand.

"It's funny, though it may be a moot point anyway. Kenny's been missing for about three weeks." George raised an eyebrow at her.

"Really?" he asked. "You seem a bit relieved as opposed to worried. Where do you think he is?"

"I wasn't worried; he's taken off before, usually just a couple of days. I didn't even file the report. His boss did. The cops came by and asked me questions. I told them I figured he'd just come stumbling in at any time. Then he didn't, and I *did* feel relieved, like maybe he just split forever or fell down drunk in a ditch and died. I almost got horrified at the fantasies I was having about his disappearance, but then I'd feel a pain in my shoulder from where he'd twisted my arm and I'd think of something even more disturbing." Abby shuddered a little bit. "Okay, maybe now we can talk about something else."

"Yes, of course, darling." George cast a quick glance at the suit of armor and smiled. "The last thing I can say on the matter is that hopefully he doesn't pop back up. He should stay gone wherever he is, and you should move on."

"I'm so glad to have you back, George. I think you're just what I need to do that." She kissed him quickly on the lips and smiled at him. "But right now I have to be going. I gotta go check on Momma." She stood and he stood with her, embracing her fiercely one more time.

"I'm glad to be back, Abby. Now let's get you home." They exited the room and Kenny watched as they left.

George returned alone an hour later and walked straight up to the suit of armor, peering into the face mask, smiling at it.

"You see, Mr. Bartlett? That's how you treat a lady. With respect, kindness and attention. They are your world, you are not theirs! You should grovel on your knees before them for their affection! A lesson, I'm afraid, you should have learned a long time ago." George patted the suit of armor on the chest. He walked out of the room and turned out the light. "Goodnight, ol' buddy. See you tomorrow."

Over the next week, George and Abby would get together every night at George's house for dinner and conversation to try to help Abby heal and move past the still missing Kenny Bartlett. Sometimes the conversation would get heated. Not between them, but only on Abby's behalf as George encouraged her to release all of her feelings and aggressions about the man who had controlled her the past few years. All while that man was watching, unmoving and unseen inside the suit of armor. Every other day, George would open the armor and attend to his captive: changing the colostomy bag, ensuring the delivery of the paralytic drug and nutrients was uninterrupted.

One day, during one of these maintenance procedures, George didn't attach the drug pack quite securely enough to the IV drip built into the suit. When he closed the armor, the connections came undone and the drug stopped flowing. As a result, some of the drugs effect had started to wear off. As the day wore on, Kenny found that he could move some of his facial muscles slightly. After a few more tries, he was able to produce a barely audible hum. Kenny started to get excited; parts of him were actually returning! By the time George and Abby had returned to the house for their now regular meeting, Kenny had managed to produce actual words. He would just wait until George left the room, and then would try to alert Abby to his presence. Sure enough, a few moments after coming in, George left Abby on the couch across the room from the suit of armor and went into the kitchen to start preparing that evening's meal. When George made it into the kitchen he switched on a radio in there, "Another One Bites The Dust" by Queen was playing. Kenny could hear the pots and pans start their ritual clanging, and then, when he was sure that only Abby would hear him, he tried to get her attention.

"Aaaaabb-eeeeee," Kenny breathed. She didn't hear him. He tried again, this time a little harder and louder. She turned her head towards the suit of armor. He did it again and saw her narrow her eyes a little bit. Kenny listened to the sounds coming from the kitchen; George was still busy cooking. He breathed at Abby once again, and this time she got up off the couch and crossed the room. She walked up to the suit of armor and looked into the face. Any holes in the face mask seemed to have been covered from the inside, so all she could see was black. She lifted the face mask to get a better look inside and saw Kenny staring back at her.

"Abby! Thank God!" he whispered. "You have to get me out of here! This psycho has had me drugged here for a month!" Abby looked back at Kenny and said nothing. She finally opened the top of the suit of armor to get a look. Kenny had lost a lot of weight. She could see where the colostomy bag had been surgically attached, where the IV drip was built into the suit of armor and where it was attached to his arm. She also saw where the drip had become detached from the cord that led to Kenny's arm.

"Please, honey, you have to get me out of here. I'm sorry for everything. Baby, please, get help or something, call the cops, I don't know. Just get me out of here!" Kenny whispered fiercely. Abby looked Kenny in the eye then dropped her gaze back to the dangling IV. She picked up the two disconnected ends and then, while looking Kenny in the eye again, connected them.

"No! No! Abby! I'm sorry! Imsurry...Isrry. Unnggghhh...." Kenny fell silent as the drugs swirled in his system again. Abby continued to look him in the eye as she closed the suit of armor and dropped the facemask, sealing Kenny in. Before she turned away to return to the couch she smiled at Kenny and blew him a kiss.

"Abby, love, I'm about ready to plate, are you ready to eat?" George asked from the kitchen. The song on the radio had changed to "Supergirl" by Reamonn.

"Yes, sweet. Ready when you are." George entered the room with two plates of food and set them on the glass table in front of the couch. He went back to the kitchen to fetch the wine and glasses; when he did Abby stood once more and faced the kitchen.

"George, darling, I have something for you in here." George re-entered the room with the wine.

"Yes, love, what's that?" he asked. As he did so, Abby dropped her dress to the ground and stood in front of George, naked, with the exception of her heels. George set the wine and glasses down on the table and went to Abby. She wrapped herself around him.

"Are you sure you're ready for this?" he asked her. She kissed him fully on the mouth, sticking her tongue in and giving him his answer. He set her gently on the couch, and then took off his shirt as she undid his belt and pants. He was already hard by the time his pants hit the ground. He took her right there on the couch, gently at first then increasing in speed and force as she commanded him to do so. She dug her nails into his back and scratched as he continued to pleasure her as Kenny never had in all his drunken fumbling. Little rivulets of blood came from these scratches, but George didn't seem to mind in the least. They made love on the couch while the food got cold, the wine untouched. They kept the same position the entire time, every time George tried to switch, Abby prevented it. George wanted to look Kenny in the eyes, but Abby kept him with his back to the suit of armor. George didn't mind that either, Kenny would be able to see the full act from his vantage point, so he stopped struggling to switch positions and kept as Abby wanted him. Abby then pulled him in even closer so his face was practically buried in the couch. His thrusts increased as he reached climax, bringing her even closer to her own. He started to shudder and cried out in pleasure as he exploded inside of her, and she let out a satisfied moan of her own. As she did, she looked dead into the facemask of the suit of armor, and winked.

154

Endless Love

David and Janet Pierce had been married five years at the time of the accident. Their courtship had been a whirlwind: they had met at the Sac-n-Pac when they bumped carts in the produce aisle, both reaching for the last bag of chopped romaine lettuce. David relinquished the bag, Janet had taken it demurely, David looked over her cart and spied that it was filled with single serving foods, much the same as his own. Never having been a bold man, David took a chance anyway and asked her out to dinner. She timidly accepted and they finished their shopping together, learning a little about each other in the process. He was 32, an English teacher at the high school, collected rare books and was a huge Pearl Jam fan. She was 30, a librarian, collected anything cat, and was a huge fan of Ella Fitzgerald. She made a joke about being a crazy cat lady in training, he laughed deeply and richly. It was a sound she could get used to hearing, she thought. They went through the checkout line (her first, of course), and exchanged phone numbers in the parking lot on the way to their respective vehicles. David drove away quite impressed with himself; Janet drove away a nervous wreck: she hadn't been in a relationship for years, or even on a date, for that matter. She wasn't even sure why she had said yes. It seemed that her mouth and brain were in collusion against her to get her back in the dating world. Either way, she had said yes and meant to keep her word, nervous or not. She went home and picked out a conservative but playful outfit; he went home and selected a snappy set of trousers and a long-sleeve button up shirt, but no tie and groomed his five o' clock shadow. She wore her hair in a ponytail most times but tonight she let it flow over her shoulders; he put a little spike to his with some hair product. They took separate cars as a precaution, and met at the restaurant at eight in the evening. A little Italian bistro that she had never been to, but he was friends with the owners. They took their time ordering, sipping on wine and getting to know each other more: both his and her parents were deceased and they were both only children. When they finally did order dinner, she chose the ricotta cheese stuffed ravioli and he chose the eggplant parmesan, with him ordering for the both of them in perfect Italian. They talked some more until the entrées arrived. She learned about some of his world travels in his search for rare books, which he couldn't afford on a teacher's salary but was funded through the inheritance that his parents left him. He learned that she wasn't as well travelled; she had never even left the state much less the country. They continued to have light conversation as they ate. She agreed that the food was marvelous. He said that each item on the menu was better than the last, having sampled them all at one time or another. They boxed up their leftovers and chatted some more over an after dinner coffee. They were the last couple in the place. She was already sure in her mind that this was a relationship that was going to continue and hoped he felt likewise. His thoughts were much the same and he asked her on a second date before the first was finished. She agreed, as long as they came back to the same restaurant. He obliged, and they closed out their check, with him leaving a generous tip that was customary. He walked her to her car and told her he was glad he took a chance for a change. She echoed his sentiment then punctuated it with a kiss. It wasn't a long, deep one. Just enough for him to know she meant it and that things were already moving in the right direction. He bade her goodnight and watched her drive away, then got in his own car and made the journey home.

The second date was as successful as the first, with the difference being they arrived in one car. He had picked her up, opening the door for her every time it was necessary, a trait that would continue throughout their relationship. At the end of the date he drove her home and she invited him in. He didn't leave until the following morning. This would be their routine for the next few weeks, dinner at the bistro, maybe a movie or a trip to the bookstore afterward, and then to her house for intense love-making sessions that would leave them in a sweaty, satisfied tangled human heap where they would fall asleep in each other's embrace. She finally asked him to move in after about a month, and he asked her to be his wife a month after that. It was a small ceremony: Lucio, the owner of the bistro stood in as David's best man and walked Janet down the aisle as well. Susan Detmer, one of Janet's co-workers, was maid-of-honor, and outside of a few witnesses from their social circle, that was it. For their honeymoon they went to Puerto Vallarta. They would go back there every year for their anniversary. Their relationship was of true love and it showed everywhere they went. They didn't go overboard on the public displays of affection, but they didn't need to. To look at them was to see a couple infatuated with each other.

The night of the accident they were returning from Lucio's. Neither one of them had had any wine with dinner that night; they had an early morning planned and didn't want even the slightest of hangovers mucking up the business. The same couldn't be said for the driver who hit them: that guy was loaded to the gills on MD 20/20, or "Mad Dog" as the kids liked to call it. They were only about three blocks from home when the drunk nodded off at the wheel and blew through a stop sign, catching David and Janet's car by the tail end, spinning and flipping it on its roof. David managed to free himself from the driver's side. A few people had come to their aid helped him to the side of the road. He told them he had to go back for Janet but, before he could get back to the car, it exploded and sent him reeling backwards. There was nothing that could be done for Janet. Ironically, he heard "Last Kiss" by Pearl Jam coming from one of the Good Samaritans cars as he sat there and watched his wife burn.

There would be no viewing at the funeral. The coroner said that Janet's body was too badly burned and a closed casket would be in David's best interest. He agreed solemnly and picked out a modest casket, something he knew Janet would have liked. In truth, the coroner was advising a closed casket because he had lost Janet's body. He wasn't sure if there was a mix-up in the paperwork, or if his slacker, stoner nephew put her body in the wrong box, again, but since she was so badly burned (that part was true), it made it easier to pull the "closed casket" routine on the husband. The funeral service itself was almost as small an affair as their wedding. Lucio was there, as their de facto father, Susan Detmer came, as well as the rest of Janet's co-workers and some of the teachers from the high school that knew her from the library. All of the mourners gathered around Janet's grave for the service except for one, David noticed. This particular griever was about fifty yards away, observing the service but not joining it. The mourner was female, David also noticed, and built strikingly similar to his Janet. This woman had blond, close-cropped hair, though, not like Janet's long brunette locks. But the height similarities were there, as well as body shape and size. David made up his mind to find out who this mourner was and why she didn't want to join the rest. As soon as the service was completed, David excused himself from the rest of the mourners and gave chase to the woman who bore a resemblance to Janet. She'd had a fifty yard head start on him, but he managed to catch up to her with only a light jog.

"Excuse me, Miss?" David said. She stopped and turned around, looking at him through big, round sunglasses.

"Yes?" she replied. The resemblance to Janet was unmistakable; her voice was even the same. The only difference was the hair and the skin tone, this woman was a few shades lighter than the tan that Janet had been.

"I was just curious as to why you didn't join the rest of us graveside?"

"Well, I wasn't invited and I didn't want to intrude..."

"It's no intrusion, but I have to ask, are you family? Because you look just like her."

"Yes, I'm her twin sister, Jennifer."

"She told me she was an only child. I wasn't aware she had a sister or I would have invited you. How come she never mentioned you?"

"It could be a myriad of reasons; we had a falling out many years ago that we never repaired."

"Still, I think she would have mentioned you at some point..." Jennifer just shrugged. David looked her up and down, marveling at how identical Jennifer was to her sister, which made him start to think about Janet again and brought some fresh tears to his eyes. He wiped them away absent-mindedly and before he knew it, was inviting her to the wake. She started to refuse, but he said he wouldn't take no for an answer.

The wake was at the couple's house. It didn't last long as only about half of the mourners showed up. There were a couple of whispers between Janet's co-workers about the newly discovered Jennifer, but that was as eventful as it got. The mourners paid their final condolences to David and left one-by-one, except Jennifer, whom David had invited to stick around after to chat more about her sister. She agreed, she wasn't due to leave until the next day on a train. David invited her to stay overnight to save her money on a hotel room. She accepted that as well, thanking him for his kindness and remarking how she saw what her sister had seen in him. They talked long into the night (well, he talked and she listened) about Janet and their all-too-brief time together. Jennifer tried to console him the best she could, and he thanked her for being there and listening. They finally went to sleep at about one in the morning: him in the bed he and Janet used to share, Jennifer on the couch in the living room. The next morning, David awoke to the smells of food, and for an instant forgot that it wasn't Janet doing the cooking. He walked out to the kitchen, half-groggy and expected Janet to be at the stove like he had grown accustomed to. He saw Jennifer, however, and though she resembled her sister almost exactly, David couldn't fool himself into thinking it was Janet. He sat at the table and thanked her for cooking; she thanked him again for the hospitality. They ate breakfast together in the dining room, and then Jennifer stated she had to go. David offered to call her a cab, but she said she had already reserved one while he was still sleeping and it would be picking her up in fifteen minutes. She used the restroom one final time and gave him a quick hug. He asked her if they could keep in touch. She said she could try, but that it would be difficult with her daily life. She left him an e-mail address to write to (she didn't like to use phones, she said) and then she was gone. David sat at the kitchen table for another fifteen minutes after she left, thinking about Janet.

It turns out they did keep in touch, though. David waited about three days after she left to send the first e-mail to which she responded almost immediately. The e-mails started and remained friendly for the first few weeks: him checking on her and her listening to him when he wanted to talk about Janet. A month after the e-mail exchange began, he asked her to come and see him. She declined initially, said she was too busy with work, but then changed her mind a day later and said that she had time in her schedule for a day trip. He met her at the library where Janet used to work. They talked about books and he found out she was a book editor back home. She said she'd love to see his collection of rarities, something she hadn't seen when she'd spent the night after the wake. They left the library and had a quick meal at Lucio's. Lucio wasn't there; he was procuring some seafood in the city. They left Lucio's and went to David's now bachelor pad. Since Janet's passing, he had moved his library of rarities to the front room, and had moved all of her things into the spare room. Some of it was boxed up, stacked orderly in the corner with "JANET" written in big black letters on them. Other things were haphazardly strewn about the room, like David had picked it up and had no idea what to do with it and laid it back down randomly. He didn't take Jennifer into this room, though, the door stayed closed and they remained in the front room. They talked about the rare books, where he had gotten some of them, and then he started to point out the books that he and Janet had purchased together. Although he didn't take on a depressed tone, she could tell his mood changed a little. Jennifer stopped him midsentence with a finger to his lips and grabbed his face gently, bringing it to hers. She kissed him lightly and gauged his reaction. He resisted at first, then closed his eyes and allowed her. She kissed him fully and closed her eyes as well, never knowing when the tears started to flow from his eyes.

He couldn't take her to the bed he had shared with Janet, so they did it right there on the floor in the front room, with his precious rarities as an audience. It was sweaty, passionate sex and he only called her Janet once. She heard him, but said nothing, continuing her rhythmic undulations on top of him. It lasted for a few minutes, and then it was over. She kissed him lightly on the mouth and stood up, reassembling her wardrobe and re-dressing herself. He just laid there and breathed with his eyes closed. She finished dressing and knelt down next to him, kissing him once more, this time on the cheek.

"I hope that helped," she said to him. She stood up, turned around and exited the front door, closing it gently behind her.

"Thank you," he said after the door was already shut, and she was already gone.

When he e-mailed her next, he was afraid she wasn't going to respond. But she did later that same day. He thanked her again, this time so she would know, and she suggested that she visit before he could even ask. He also didn't hesitate to agree and asked where she'd like to meet. She said she would come straight to the house; they could go wherever after that. They set it up for the next day. This time, she was barely through the door before their clothes were off and they were on the floor, doing the horizontal boogie. He didn't call her Janet this time, but he thought about her the entire time. And the second time, twenty minutes after they finished their first session.

They sat at the dining room table, the afternoon sun shining through the window and playing on the floor. He'd made a light lunch for the both of them, not even realizing that he cut the crusts of the bread off the sandwiches, just like Janet liked. They ate in silence and, when they were finished, the silence remained for a bit before they both spoke at the same time.

"I have to tell you something," they said in unison. David laughed his deep, rich laugh, the one that Janet thought she could hear for the rest of her life.

"Ladies first," he said.

"No, no, you. It looks like something has been troubling you for a bit now. If it'll help you, go ahead." David drew in a deep breath and held it for a few seconds, before exhaling slowly and beginning.

"I had been alone for a long while before I met Janet. When we met, it was like an instant attraction. If we had been cartoon characters, there would have been lightning bolts shooting back and forth between us. That's how electric it felt to me. I knew from the start that she and I were to be together and I knew she knew it, too. Our time together was the best thing I've ever experienced. Far better than any place I've seen or book I've acquired, even the ones we got together, because those are just books, I can replace those, and those were just places I can see again. But she's gone. I can't see her again. Then you come along, and I enjoy my time with you, and everything that you do, but when I look at you I don't see Jennifer, I see Janet. I'm using you as a surrogate for her, and that's not fair to you. I can be with you, and maybe have a relationship with you, but I'm afraid all I'll ever see is Janet, and you deserve to be seen as Jennifer. I could love you, but it would be for the wrong reasons." With this finally off of his chest, David's head sank and he looked at his hands that were clasped in his lap.

"That's about it," he said quietly. Jennifer looked at him from across the table and smiled a kind smile at him, tears welling up in her eyes.

"That's one of the reasons I fell in love with you in the first place, David, always putting others above yourself." He looked up from his lap at her, and had a few tears in his own eyes.

"In the first place, what do you mean...?"

"It's me, David. It's Janet." David blinked a couple of times and said nothing. She looked back at him patiently. Finally he said something.

"Look, Jennifer, you...I mean, Jan...this isn't funny."

"I'm not joking," she said, kindly. "I'm Janet, and it's time you learned the truth. I was born three hundred and forty-three years ago. From what I can tell, I cannot die." David listened and said nothing as she continued. "I think the car accident is the closest I've come to dying, I actually had to grow back new skin and hair, hence the lightness of my pigmentation, and the shortness of my hair at the funeral." David finally spoke up.

"But your hair, her hair, Janet's hair, was brunette; you're obviously a natural blond..."

164

"I used to get my hair done by the Koreans," she said sheepishly, "and you never saw any hair, um, down there, so it was the one and only thing I hid from you."

"Not the only thing, apparently. So, what are you, like Sean Connery in Highlander or something? 'There can be only one!'?" Now she was looking at her lap.

"As far as I know, I *am* the only one. It's why I stopped getting into relationships. It's hard to maintain a solid relationship with a person who doesn't grow old with you. I hadn't been with anybody for over a hundred years before I met you, it was too painful for everyone involved. But then I met you, and you're right, it was electric. I knew I had to be with you, even if it was brief, even if you didn't grow old with me, even if it was doomed like all the rest of them. After the accident I was going to stay away, make a clean break and start over again, and this time I vowed that I wouldn't get anywhere near a relationship. But I missed you. So I devised this 'twin sister' scheme to have you in my life again." She sighed deeply when she finished and continued to look at her lap. David pushed back from the table and went to Janet. He knelt next her and looked up at her downturned face, smiling.

"I want you to come with me," he said to her. He grasped her by the hand and directed her outside, to the back yard. In the back yard was a large tree; in the tree was an old tree house the previous owners had built for their kids decades ago. David and Janet had been in it once when they first moved into the house, and it had been rickety then, having become unstable with the growing of the tree. Now, more than five years later, it was practically condemnable. This didn't stop David from scrambling up the tree and into the tree house. Janet winced with trepidation watching him.

165

"Ooh, be careful," she warned. He popped out to what should have been a balcony on the tree house, now it was just some gnarled wood with half a railing attached to it. She could hear the wood protest under his weight as he stood on it.

"Be careful, David," she warned again. As if to mock her, he stood at the edge of the half railing and flapped his arms like they were wings. She heard the wood groan again and cringed. He was still smiling like a loon, and she had no idea why.

"Why should I be careful, darling?" he called down to her. Before she could answer he jumped up and down on the old, rotting tree house wood. The tree shook and the tree house shifted. The entire works came crashing down, David included. Janet let out a little yelp of surprise and watched as her recently grieving widower fell from the tree and was buried under wood and rusty nails and then it got quiet again. Janet broke her trance and ran to the pile of rubble and started to pull some of the rotting wood, looking for David's body. After moving a few boards, she saw him, lying tangled among the wood, neck bent at a crazy angle. She reached out to him, and as she did, he opened his eyes and flashed her that loon smile.

"Why should I be careful, darling?" he asked again. "I was born in 1816." He then started to laugh that laugh of his, the one that Janet would get to hear for the rest of her life.

The Guy Next Door

The walls of my apartment are pretty thin, as are the ceilings and floors, I surmise. You get what you pay for, the saying goes. My income isn't grand by any means, so at $599 a month, in this economy, I should be happy to have four walls and a roof at all. The floor-plan of the apartment is as such: the front door opens to the living room area, which segues into the dining area on the left side and that faces an enclosed kitchen. Beyond the kitchen/dining area is the hallway that leads to the master (and only) bedroom. Halfway down this hallway, on the same side as the kitchen, is the bathroom. The only windows are located at the front and back:

there's a big, bay window positioned next to the front door and there's a small, sliding window in the back bedroom that's located at about eye level. I mostly keep to myself; I have a job where I'm required to be up long before the rest of the normal world, and am home usually before the kids are out of school. As such, my sleep patterns are opposite most everyone else's: I crash soon after I get home in the afternoon, wake up in the late evening and, around two in the morning, hi-ho, it's off to work I go. I wave at Mrs. Covarrubias when she's walking her dog or we pass each other on the way to the mailboxes, but I only know her because I got her mail one time. We don't stop and chat or anything, just the wave. I don't think she speaks English, anyway. She lives in the apartment above mine; she's a small woman, and quiet, luckily her dog is, too. To my right (or your left, if you're facing my door), is who I call "Tetsuo", but I don't know his real name. He's an Asian guy, and he reminds me of Tetsuo from the movie "Akira", well, before he got all metamorphosed and stuff. I've only seen him a couple of times, and I've never talked to him. He looks like he might speak English, but in this town...well; it's a real melting pot. You really can't make assumptions based on looks alone. I only passed judgment on Mrs. Covarrubias' language skills based on the way she answered the door when I brought her mail over that one time. Anyway, above Tetsuo is The Manager, then next to Mrs. Covarrubias is Hector, the maintenance man, and underneath him, to my left (or your right, if you're facing my door) is empty. This smoking hot blonde used to live there, up until a number of weeks ago. I tried to talk to her once when I was coming home from work, but she was in a hurry, so the conversation didn't last long. I got her name, Krista, she got mine, Gary; said a little nice-to-meetcha-neighbor and well-gotta-run, and I never got the chance to speak to her again. I could hear plenty of her through the wall, but it wasn't like eavesdropping or spying, more like hearing someone trying to talk to you underwater.

170

I could hear her voice, but not make out what she was saying. Usually it was probably just some animated conversation with a girlfriend, or relative, most times I would just tune it out. She did like to turn her music up, though, so I got very well educated in the works of Katy Perry. I skew more toward the Slayer spectrum of the music scale, but I will say, that Perry chick can sing. I actually kind of liked that "Waking Up In Vegas" song. Anyway, about, oh, three weeks after the small talk we had, I noticed that I hadn't heard anything from the other side of the wall. I didn't really think much of it at the time, I figured she'd just moved out, that her lease was up and I didn't give it much thought after that.

The apartment stayed empty for almost the whole month, and then one day, after I had just gotten home, I heard The Manager's voice, talking to someone. I casually looked out the peephole and saw The Manager coming up the sidewalk from the leasing office, with him was a larger man, at least a foot taller than The Manager, and twice as wide. He was wearing a dark blue New York Yankees ball cap, with the brim pulled slightly down to shade his already sunglass clad eyes. He had dark stubble on his jaw, probably more than a few days growth. Rough, black hair poked out from underneath the cap, and grew down in the back to cover the nape of his neck. His muscular, upper frame bore a t-shirt that may have been a size too small for him; it strained against physique, one he had been clearly working on for a while. The t-shirt was black, and adorned with what looked like a regular old smiley face, but on closer inspection, there was a bloody bullet hole right between the eyes of the smiley face. His lower half looked to be dressed in black cargo pants, with what appeared to be combat boots on his feet. For some reason, he looked like a Gunnar to me. They walked past my apartment, and I switched my view from the peephole to the window, looking through the blinds stealthily, so as not to be seen. I heard The

Manager giving the spiel about the rent and the utilities and then they were inside the vacant apartment, where just a few weeks ago Krista was singing "I Kissed A Girl" and I liked it. There was no doubt in my mind that this new fellow, were he to take the place, would not be listening to any of the fine works of Ms. Perry.

Gunnar did end up taking the place, and for the first few days I heard nothing. No voices, no music, nothing. I knew he had taken the place because I saw the U-Haul dropping stuff off, and heard them moving *that* in, but it was silent after that. Just when I thought that Gunnar was going to be the model neighbor, I did start to hear sounds. There was the unmistakable sounds of grunting and of metal clanking together, my mind crafted a hilarious cartoon image of Gunnar as a blacksmith, grunting and striking his hammer down on his forge, all while wearing his smiley face t-shirt. I shook the image off and listened closer, and discovered what the sound truly was. Gunnar was lifting weights. He apparently kept his well-crafted physique sculpted at home. This was understandable, given the amount that a lot of these workout places charged for memberships and whatnot. I had entered a contest one time for a free membership to one of these places, and was excited when I won, until I figured out that pretty much everybody won. That was how they got you in there, a month's free membership when you signed up for six. Anyway, I'm getting off subject. I could hear Gunnar working out next door, and while it wasn't loud, it was consistent. We seemed to keep about the same hours, although I never passed him on my way out, or on my way home, I would hear him working out shortly before I'd lay down for bed, and he'd still be at it when I woke up for work later on. I'd only hear it when I was in the living room, and if it got too bothersome I'd just slap on my headphones and jam out to some Ministry or KMFDM while I surfed on my computer, or I'd just plug in to the computer itself and listen to it. I didn't have a TV, didn't feel the need for one. Anything I wanted to watch I could find on the internet, so as long as I kept my connection going, my computer was my TV. Anyway, that's pretty much all I ever heard over there, and after about a few weeks' time, it got to where I'd just tune it out and wouldn't need the headphones anymore.

One night, about a month after Gunnar had moved in, I was riding the bus to work. I normally get off the bus at a stop that is just a block away from the building I work in. Instead I got off a stop earlier because it was in front of a convenience store. This particular evening, I hadn't had my usual wake-up coffee at my apartment before leaving to catch the bus. My coffee maker had decided to give up the ghost, and would brew no more. So I got off the bus and went in to the store, and readied my cup of coffee. I took it to the counter where Habib (probably not his real name) was tending store and set it down while he rang me up. He asked me if I'd like anything else, some beef jerky, perhaps and I said no and he gave me my total: ninety four cents. I fished the change out of my pocket and gave him two quarters, three dimes, a nickel and nine pennies. While Habib proceeded to count it to the penny, I looked around absentmindedly at the flyers and notices that people had tacked to a corkboard at the front of the counter. It was a random smattering of garage sales and handyman services and a whole host of landscaping companies and tree trimming services with Mexican surnames. Habib was putting the change from the sale in the cash register as I turned to go, when one more notice on the corkboard caught my eye. It was a "missing person" flyer, with the obligatory big block letters in black and red that screamed MISSING and REWARD and CALL POLICE WITH INFORMATION. In the center of the flyer was a picture of a pretty blonde, all smiles and blue eyes. I didn't need to look at the name on the flyer to know that I recognized the girl in the picture, but I looked anyway. Underneath the picture, but above REWARD was the name KRISTA MICHELLE HOLLOWAY.

Thousands of people come up missing every year, but it had never happened to someone I knew personally. I took the flyer with me, after getting Habib's permission (I was surprised that he didn't charge me for it), folded it up and put it in my pocket. I would think about her all throughout work that night, remembering our brief conversation, recalling her singing. When I got home the following afternoon, I took the flyer out and stuck it to the refrigerator with a novelty magnet shaped like a pineapple. I looked at it for a few minutes and thought to myself if maybe I'd tried harder, tried to talk to her more, that maybe somehow I could have kept her safe. I began to feel a bit of guilt creep in and decided then and there that I would try to help find out what had happened to her. I didn't fancy myself a detective or anything, although I'd read my fair share of Encyclopedia Brown and The Three Investigators books when I was a kid, and now liked to watch Law and Order and CSI on my computer, but I just wanted to help somehow. Maybe get a little perspective from someone not as closely tied to the case. Instead of going to bed that day, I went to my computer and started to research the disappearance of Krista Holloway. I already knew from the flyer the day she had gone missing, what the flyer didn't tell me were the little details. I read every article I could find from the local paper, and because she was a young, pretty, blonde, white girl, there was a fair amount of national news exposure as well. I watched all the CNN reports, the Headline News coverage, even stomached some of the awful FOX News. I had my notepad pulled up on my laptop and typed in notes as I watched the videos and read the articles. After a couple of hours of research, I knew what she was wearing when she disappeared, when and where she was last seen, all the pertinent details. I looked over my notes and saved the file, suddenly feeling the exhaustion. I closed my computer and stretched, on the other side of the wall I heard the grunt and clank of Gunnar working out, and wished I could hear Katy Perry just one more time.

The next couple of days I couldn't focus, either while I was at work or at home. When I was working, my mind kept returning to that picture on the flyer, her smile. When I was at home I'd have my computer open, with my notes onscreen and I'd pace around, stopping occasionally to look at the notes, and then pace some more. I was frustrated that I couldn't come up with anything more, and the notes were giving me nothing. I couldn't go in the kitchen and look at the flyer and not feel like I was failing her. I decided to take some vacation time from work, I had a few weeks built up and it would allow me to do one of two things: either I would find a way to let this all go and accept I had done all I could for her, or I was going to throw myself headlong in to it and get some answers. My head was set on the former, but my heart made me do the latter. The first day of my vacation I took her missing flyer around to the neighbors that were living there when she was, which meant The Manager, Tetsuo, Hector and Mrs. Covarrubias. I went to The Manager first, he would know the most, I assumed, because he had to flip the apartment of the missing person. When I talked to him, he told me that after she had gone missing her family had come in to clean her place out, since missing people can't pay rent. Apparently this had been done during one of the mornings I was at work. I thought that was kind of harsh, but understood he still had a business to run. He said the family had given him little information, so he had little to give me in return. I talked to Hector next, since he was the one that had to let the police in to investigate, the family in to collect her things and the one to make sure there was no damage to the apartment when all was said and done. He said there was nothing out of the ordinary anytime he went there, and didn't get any info from the police or the family, just kept quiet and out of the way. I went to Tetsuo next, and got absolutely nothing out of him. That left Mrs. Covarrubias, so I went to her apartment and knocked on the door, steeling myself for the language barrier. The door cracked open slightly and she peered out at me, wincing against the sunlight.

"Si?" she asked. I started slowly with my limited Spanish.

"Hablo Ingles?" I asked.

"Yes, you speak English," she said. I put my limited Spanish away.

"Whew, I thought you only spoke Spanish," I said. I proceeded to ask her about Krista, and showed her the flyer like I did with all the others. She told me she remembered the girl, had seen her on the day she disappeared. I asked her where, and she paused for a moment. Through the crack in the door I could smell Mrs. Covarrubias' apartment. It smelled of cinnamon and old lady perfume. When she finally spoke, she told me where she had seen Krista: at the market down the street. I asked her at what time and she told me, it was after the time the cops had established as for when she had went missing. My heart started racing, I had a fresh lead. And I knew a cashier at the market who could probably get me access to the security tapes. I thanked Mrs. Covarrubias and made tracks down to the market.

I talked to my buddy and told him what was up; he said he'd be more than happy to let me look as long as he got his name in the papers with mine. I wasn't worried about fame or fortune; I wanted justice for a girl I hardly knew, but was haunted by. I asked him how far the tapes were backed up to, and he said they had switched over to a computerized system a year ago, so everything since then was stored and catalogued on a hard drive, all I had to do was put in a day and time and the computer would do the rest. I gave him the information that Mrs. Covarrubias had given me and he punched it into the computer. There were four cameras total, and he put all four views on the monitor at once. Krista came into view of one of the cameras seconds after we started watching. She was wearing the outfit she would disappear in, and she appeared to be alone, picking out a few items here and there. Nothing seemed to be out of the ordinary, and I was afraid that my new lead would prove to be a bust. I continued to watch her finish her shopping and she got in line to pay for her purchases, using the express lane for 15 items or less. I watched her make small talk with the little old lady at the register, whose glasses were so thick I was immediately reminded of Professor Farnsworth from "Futurama". She was finishing her transaction when someone got in line behind Krista and my already racing heart leapt into my throat. I had only seen him through my peephole and briefly through the blinds of my front window, but I knew immediately that it was Gunnar in line behind Krista. He only had two items with him: a box of trash bags and a large box of plastic wrap, the kind you use to wrap your food in. Or the kind you can use to suffocate someone.

I watched Gunnar watch Krista on the screen as she finished her purchase and made her way to the exit. His transaction was completed quickly and he exited swiftly behind her. I asked my buddy if there were parking lot cameras, and he said no, they hadn't gotten that part of the package. The owners were more concerned with what on in the store than outside of it. I felt a sense of frustration at this, surely if there had been parking lot cameras there would have been some evidence of Gunnar either abducting Krista, or following her, something. All kinds of other questions started swirling in my mind: had he planned this? Did he stalk her with the intent to take her and kill her and move in to her apartment like some kind of homicidal hermit crab? Was this an impulse thing? It seemed like I had more questions than answers now that I had seen this tape, and I went home, spent. I went to the kitchen and looked into Krista's blue eyes. She smiled back at me, pleased that I had made some progress. But it wasn't enough, and I knew it. I leaned my head against the fridge on the flyer and closed my eyes. I knew what I had to do next, and I didn't like it. I ate a sandwich thoughtlessly and tastelessly, I needed something in my belly. I wanted to wobble off to bed after that, but before I did I went to the front room and looked at the wall that separated me from my neighbor. I could hear him working out over there; he was really going at it. I narrowed my eyes at the wall and raised my fist at it, shaking it as I did. I was going to make Gunnar pay, but I needed more proof.

The second day of my vacation should have been spent taking what I knew to the cops, to let them in on the footage I'd uncovered and give them a suspect in Gunnar. Maybe the outcome would have been different. I don't know. All I know is I didn't go to the cops, I didn't give them a suspect, and I broke into Gunnar's that day. I needed to have my proof. I woke up around 8 o' clock after having dreams of Krista: I'm behind her in the check-out line and she turns to me and smiles, just as Gunnar snatches her up and runs out the door. I want to go after them, but I can't get out of the check-out line, the old lady won't let me leave without paying, and I have no money. I came to in a sweat, the dream fading as they always do. I went out to the kitchen to make a coffee and remembered I still hadn't replaced the old one yet. I still had time to go down to the market to pick a cheap one up; they had a couple of different models. I dressed in jeans and a t-shirt advertising The

Genitorturers. I strolled to the market and picked out a decent model for about twenty bucks. I went to the registers, but avoided the express lane with the old lady. The dream had faded, but that part stayed fresh. I took my purchase home, and was walking down the sidewalk leading to my door, when Gunnar exited his and nearly ran me and my coffee maker over. He barely paid me any notice, just locked his door and strode off down the sidewalk without a "Sorry", "Excuse Me", or "Fuck You Very Much". I scurried inside and locked the door behind me, heart pounding. I took the coffee maker to the kitchen and brewed up a strong pot. After a couple of cups, the caffeine had me amped up and ready to go. I went outside and went behind our building. If the windows were all the same, with the same locking mechanism, then I would be able to get in to any of the windows. One time I had locked myself out of my apartment, I know, stupid thing to do. Anyway, I had come around the back after failing to open the front window, and found I could jimmy the latch on the window, after about three minutes of work I was in and it was problem solved. Now I hoped to apply this knowledge to getting into someone else's apartment. I peered up into Gunnar's back window and he indeed had the same latch as I did. I went to work on it and it came open quicker than mine had, it was much looser. I slid the window open and hoisted myself up and in. I was now standing in Gunnar's bedroom.

It was sparsely furnished: a twin bed with one pillow, a three drawer dresser, and a night stand with an old-fashioned alarm clock on it. The ceiling had a fan with a light in it, so there was no need for an extra lamp back here. I slid the window closed and advanced in the darkened room, eyes adjusting. The door to the room was closed so I went to it and opened it, peering out. There was a dim light on in the front room that cast a long shadow down the hallway. I exited the bedroom and made my way down the hallway.

The bathroom was spotless, no proof in there. The kitchen was equally clean, the only thing out of the ordinary was the massive amounts of protein powders this guy had. I went into the front room and it was the sparsest of all. There was a weight bench next to the wall we shared and across the room was a wall mounted TV with a DVD player attached to it. There was a pile of DVDs next to the player, but they all turned out to be workout videos, and not even the sexy kind. There was one place I hadn't looked, and that was the bedroom closet. I would check that out and if I didn't find anything I was out of there. I retraced my steps back to the bedroom and closed the door behind me. I went to the walk-in closet and went in. I was just starting to look around when I heard the front door open and Gunnar came home. I froze in the closet, not knowing what to do. I could feel my pulse in my ears but I could still hear that he wasn't alone. There was a female voice with him.

I couldn't make out what she was saying, but she was doing most of the talking. Then they were in the kitchen and I could hear a little more, but not much. They moved from the kitchen and I heard them thump up against the closed bedroom door. The talking had stopped; I assumed that their mouths were otherwise preoccupied. The door to the bedroom came open and the two of them tumbled in. Through the openings of the closet door I could see them, but the door was closed enough to provide me cover. He was already naked, and I could tell by the size of his Thunder-Cock ™ that he was no steroid user. I took a good look at his partner and was struck by the similarities she had to Krista. Blonde hair, blue eyes, slim figure…this guy definitely had a type. Was I looking at his next potential victim? She looked like a willing enough participant, but things could change at a moment's notice if he decided it was time to get rough. Right now, though, it was Consensual City: she was blowing him with great fervor, and he was standing there with his hands on his hips, not even forcing the issue. I watched as he finally mounted her, and I got a little aroused, but kept my cool. I had to for Krista. They finished Round 1 about seven minutes later and went out of the room to the bathroom together. I heard the shower turn on, and knew this was my chance to get the hell out of there. I peeked out of the closet door and saw the coast was clear. I slipped out of the closet and put the door back in place, and crept across to the window. I slid it open carefully, it hadn't made noise before, and I didn't want it to start now. With the window open I hoisted myself out and once outside, carefully slid the window shut. I boogied around the front of the building and ducked inside my own front door, closing it behind me and leaning my back against it, exhaling a large (but quiet) sigh. I locked the deadbolt and walked over towards the kitchen, and started to tremble as I did. I had been through all of that, and had no good news for Krista. Still, she smiled at me when I got to the kitchen, like she always did, and I put my head on her paper one. I stayed there for a minute, and then went to my bedroom and lay down. I didn't even bother to take my shoes off. I lay I my bed and thought of Krista, a woman I was sure I was now in love with, but would never get to see again. I was thinking of her when I drifted off.

I woke up after a dreamless sleep a few hours later, and it was quiet next door. It was dark out, but I didn't know what time it was. I fumbled for my cell phone on the bedside table and hit the button on it. 3:23 AM registered back at me in green digital lights. I got up and walked to the kitchen to use my new coffee maker. It brewed quickly and I took a cup with me to the front room, sat down and listened. I heard no sounds of Gunnar working out. I went to the bathroom and sat on the toilet, coffee working its magic and after about two minutes, I heard a sound from the bathroom on the opposite side of the wall. Gunnar's side of the wall. Gunnar's bathroom. The sound was the unmistakable report of a large trash bag being unfurled. You know the sound it makes: you pull it out of the box and open the mouth of it, grasping it on both sides and giving it a mighty shake to pop it open. *That* sound. That sound in and of itself would probably be of no consequence, but in its context: at 3:30 in the morning, in a bathroom, and followed by what I heard next, it seemed a little suspect. What followed next was the sound of water swirling, lots of it, most likely in the tub. Like he was washing something, or some*things* in the tub. As I sat, bare-assed on the toilet, defecation all but forgotten, I could hear him taking things out of the water, dripping things, and then there was the rustling sound of the trash bag. I could hear all of this through the wall. It sounded like he extracted about nine objects from the water and deposited them in that trash bag. My imagination raced, the first thing I thought of was the blonde from earlier, that he had done her in with the plastic wrap he purchased and was now putting her in the trash bags he had partnered in the purchase. I looked at the wall that separated our bathrooms and tried to will myself to see through the wall, but all I could see was my own imagination imprinted on it, and that was bad enough. The sounds next door ceased, and I finally got myself off the toilet. I had my coffee cup with me; I took a sip and immediately spat it out; it was cold. I had sat there so long my coffee had chilled. I went back to the kitchen and dumped out the cold coffee, then poured a fresh one. I leaned on the counter and sipped it and looked at Krista. She smiled back at me and I knew I was going back in.

If I couldn't do anything for Krista, if I couldn't find any evidence to help her out, maybe I could get him on his fresh one, the one I just heard him disposing of through the wall. As I was sipping on this new cup of coffee, I heard him open his front door. I raced to the blinds and looked through them the same way I had when he was first checking out the place. I saw him leave his place, with a large black trash bag in tow, and it looked weighted heavily down. There were a few odd angles poking out of it, but to the casual eye, it just looked like a really full trash bag. To me, it looked like it was really full of human. He locked the door behind him and slung the trash bag over his shoulder, like an anti-Santa, and strode away. I wanted to get in that bathroom and see if he might have left something to clean later, or his souvenir. All the crazies collected souvenirs; this dude would be no different. I just hadn't found them yet. I waited a few minutes to make sure he was gone, and out I went, to the back of the building again. The window was still unlocked, of course, so I was in even quicker this time. I dropped down into the darkened bedroom and moved swiftly to the door. I pressed up against it and listened briefly, I heard nothing. I opened the door and entered the hallway that was as dimly lit as before. I went to the front room first this time, and found nothing there, like before. I paused at the kitchen, and poked my head in, there were two glasses sitting on the counter with the ghosts of beverages past in them, nothing out of the ordinary there. I finally descended on my target, the bathroom. It smelled of bleach and laundry detergent, but mostly bleach. You didn't have to be a regular watcher of CSI to know that bleach got rid of LOTS of evidence. It smelled of it directly in the tub, of course it would, so I started to poke around the drain a bit. I didn't see any blood, but there were a few long, blond hairs stuck in the drain holes. I plucked them out and wrapped them in a few sheets of toilet paper and then stuck them in my front pants pocket. Satisfied that I had finally found something, I turned to leave the bathroom. As I did, I slipped on the little bath mat that was in front of the toilet and went sprawling out on the floor in the hallway. I immediately thought of "Tyler" by The Toadies right before I hit my head and blacked out.

I woke up an undetermined amount of time later; things would begin to happen so fast after that that we never determined how long I was out in Gunnar's apartment when I hit my head. I want to say it was only a few minutes, no more than ten, but like I said, we're really not sure. What we do know is this: I woke up in the hallway of Gunnar's apartment with a nasty lump on my head, and a ringing in my ears. Also, Gunnar and his blonde girlfriend, the one I had seen him plowing earlier, who most assuredly was not dead, were standing in the open front doorway, looking at me.

"Charlie, who is that?" the blonde said. I looked at her and then back at Gunn—*Charlie*, and he had advanced in to the room a little bit, peering at me in the dim light.

"I think it's the neighbor guy," Charlie said to her. Then, to me he said, loudly, "Hey, guy! What the fuck you doing in my place?" I touched my pocket to make sure I still had the hairs from the drain, and was about to say something, but I couldn't get the words out right, since I was still suffering slightly from the minor head trauma I had just received. I wanted to accuse him of Krista's disappearance and possible murder, but I couldn't even say my own name at that point. Instead I kind of just sat on the ground and looked at the two of them dumbly. I figured worst case scenario was I could pretend to be drunk and that when my key didn't work I came through the back window, but just the wrong back window. Charlie had advanced a little further in to the room and the blonde stood a few steps inside the doorway. I could see it was starting to get light outside, so it had to be around 6 AM. My next thought was that we had been causing quite the ruckus and had disturbed the neighbors, because Mrs. Covarrubias was standing outside the open door. I figured she had come to see what all the hubbub was. Charlie advanced on me a little further, and I scrambled backwards in the

184

hallway. I got my wits back about me and was about to level an accusation against Charlie when something caught my eye. I had only seen it a couple of times, and on a TV monitor, but I had it committed to memory nonetheless. Mrs. Covarrubias was standing in the doorway, dressed in the outfit that Krista had disappeared in.

Charlie was still coming at me, fists balled, oblivious that Mrs. Covarrubias was now inside of his apartment as well. I had my eyes fixed on her, Charlie had his eyes on me, and Mrs. Covarrubias had her eyes on Charlie's blonde girlfriend. This is about the time things started to seem like they were moving in slow motion. I was no longer paying attention to Charlie, I could hear him saying something but I didn't register what he said. My attention was on the now-trembling Mrs. Covarrubias. Wait, trembling isn't the right word. She was having a full-on body seizure, and then her eyes rolled back in her head. She stuck her hands and arms in the air like she was doing a one-person Wave and then her hands started to wiggle, like she was doing jazz hands. From the tips of her fingers long, black appendages began to sprout and then her hands bent back at a crazy angle. Her mouth dropped open into an elongated "O" shape and her tongue lolled out, it stopped halfway down her chest then began to inflate and turn grey. Her feet were bare, and they began to curl inward, the toes trying to meet the heels. At this point, it looked like she was losing balance, she was still shaking but kept swaying backwards until she snapped forward one time and then did a backflip, landing on the crazily bent hands that were now her feet. The outfit of Krista's that she was wearing, a cute little sundress with yellow daffodils on it, slipped down over her head when she did the 180 degree flip and was now puddled at the floor at her hands/feet. Her legs, which were now pointed in the air, were thrashing about wildly. Without the sundress on, I could see Mrs. Covarrubias' backside, all pockmarked and dimpled, and also

185

her naughty bits. Her tongue, which was now fully engorged and hanging to the floor, was being used to steady the beast as it transformed. The feet at the end of the thrashing legs weren't feet anymore, they now resembled clawed hands. The legs were bent at the knees, making a kind of "Y" formation, until the backs of the knees split open and a separate set of arms burst forth from there. I looked back at Mrs. Covarrubias' crotch, and that's when the real horror began. Her vagina split open, all the way to her anus, and her hips became shoulders as a head started to protrude. It looked like the world's ugliest baby was being born, but baby was too kind of a word for what I was seeing. The face came out, as black as the rest of the appendages, it had eight eyes on it like a spider, and large, sharp mandibles to match. There wasn't much left of the Mrs. Covarrubias that I knew, but then if this was what she really was, I really didn't know her at all. The whole transformation took maybe 5 to 6 seconds. It felt like forty years. Charlie and his lady still had no idea what was going on, until the former Mrs. Covarrubias grabbed the blonde with all four of her arms. She started shrieking, which got Charlie's attention, which was kind of lucky for me, because by that time, he had reached me and was about to punch me in the face. When his girl started to scream, Charlie gave me a confused look and turned around; when he saw what was happening he dropped his fist, and me. Mrs. Covarrubias had hoisted her in the air and brought the blonde in close. She tried to scream out Charlie's name, but only managed to get out "Ch-oontch!" as the shiny black mandibles pierced her temples and a proboscis erupted from the monster's mouth and punctured her forehead. There was a greedy, sucking sound as the creature turned the blonde into a human Slurpee. Charlie had gone slack-jawed by this point, his mind obviously recoiling in horror. I began to hear a high-pitched screaming, at first I thought it was coming from the blonde, but she was silent. The scream was coming from Charlie; it was almost comical that a sound like that was coming from a guy so big. He was backing away from the thing that looked like a spider, a lizard and a mosquito all at the same time. He must have forgotten I was there, because he kept backing up and started to squish me against the bedroom door. Realizing I was still there, he turned to me and screamed in my face.

"WHAT THE FUCK IS THAT?" he shouted.

"Mrs. Covarrubias," was my only reply. The creature was paying us no mind; it was busy enjoying its meal. I was able to get out from behind Charlie and before I knew what I was doing, I was running at the creature. I did my best impersonation of Liu Kang from Mortal Kombat and jumped in to the air, dropkicking the creature. It let go of the blonde, but it was too late for her. There was a loud "Squick!" sound as the proboscis disengaged from her skull, and the creature turned to me and roared. I had bounced off of the thing and was on the ground, looking up at it. I crab-walked backwards to where Charlie was at, or where I thought he was, but he had opened the bedroom door and was inside there somewhere. I thought he was probably making for the open window, which seemed to be the smart play. The creature started towards me, clicking its mandibles together. Charlie re-appeared and he had a large, metal dumbbell in his hand. I could see on the side that it weighed 30 pounds, but Charlie reared back his arm and threw it at the creature like it weighed no more than a baseball. It struck the creature in the face, but seemed to have little effect. The dumbbell bounced off the thing, and rolled back down the hallway a few feet. I tried to do the same thing Charlie had done with it, but when I went to pick it up, I damn near tore my shoulder out of socket. Charlie picked it up instead and threw it again, this time it hit the creature right in the middle of the face, crushing two of its eight eyes. The creature roared in pain and with inhuman speed, exited Charlie's front door. Before it left, it snatched up the dead blonde and took her with it. I could only assume that Mrs. Covarrubias, or whatever she was, was going back to her apartment. Charlie ran to the front door and slammed it shut, locking it and putting his back up against it, breathing heavily. He looked at me, eyes full of a thousand questions, but his mouth could ask none of them. We stayed like that for what seemed to be thousands of eons, but in reality was about 45 seconds and then I broke the silence.

"We have to go after it," I said. "For Krista."

"Who the fuck is Krista?" Charlie asked.

"The chick that used to live here. I thought you were the one responsible for her disappearance and possible murder. Turns out I was wrong."

"Is that how you wound up in my pad? Playing junior detective?"

"Yeah," I said, "sorry about breaking in to your place and all, I probably watch too many crime shows; my imagination kind of ran away on me. I guess it's better to leave this kind of thing to the professionals."

"We can work all that out later," he said, "right now the bigger problem is whatever the hell that was that took off with my date."

"Um, yeah, sorry about that, too. She was a pretty girl. You two been dating long?"

"Nah," he said, looking at his feet. "I just met her a few days ago at the market."

"How do you want to handle it? I think we should move fast, though, there's no telling what that thing might do. If we catch it while it's still eating, we might have a chance. Do you have any other weapons besides that dumbbell?"

"I can probably use the bar from my weight bench, but that's about it. I have a couple of kitchen knives; I don't think they're sharp enough to do any damage though."

"Well, grab the bar, it'll have to do. I have a couple of replica ninja swords at my place, I don't know how sturdy they are, but they're sharp as fuck." Charlie grabbed the bar from the weight bench after removing the weights from it. Seeing the way he'd flung that dumbbell, I almost suggested he leave the weights on it for more heft. He opened the door to his place and we looked outside. It was lighter outside than before, but there was no one stirring, and no one had come to see what the commotion was. We slipped over to my place and went inside. I fetched my swords, and then we both stood quietly in my apartment, straining to hear any noises that might be coming from the apartment upstairs. We couldn't hear anything. We made our way back outside and crept up the stairs to the second landing. The stairs to the second floor were at Charlie's end of the building. As such, we had to pass Hector's apartment before we got to Mrs. Covarrubias' door. Charlie was in front of me, brandishing the bar from the weight bench. As we were passing Hector's apartment, his door opened and he peered out, sleep still in his eyes.

"Whazz goin' on?" he asked in heavily accented English. "I heered shouteen an' screemeen. " He saw the blades in my hands and his eyes got really big. "Oh, sheet."

"Shhh," I said to him. "There's a big bug in Mrs. Covarrubias' apartment, we're going to go squash it." Hector regarded us for a second longer.

"I heered noices comeen from her *casa, tambien*. Chould I get the manayer?"

"No," I said, "but if you have a shotgun or something we could use your help."

"A chotgun?" he queried. "How big dis bug?"

"Pretty fucking big," Charlie said. We decided to fill Hector in on what happened downstairs, concerned that he wouldn't believe us, but determined to get his help. We gave him the Cliff's Notes version, and he nodded his head while he listened. It took just a couple of minutes to give him the rundown; I was pretty sure he thought we were crazy.

"*Un momento,*" Hector said and disappeared back inside his apartment. I looked at Charlie and shrugged and figured he'd gone to call the cops or the loony bin. He came back a few moments later, carrying a huge revolver and a flashlight. He looked at us and brandished the gun.

"Pest control," he said.

The three of us approached Mrs. Covarrubias' door. Charlie stood in front of it and made like he was about to kick it in. Hector stopped him, showing him the keys and putting his forefinger to his lips in the universal "Shh" gesture. Charlie nodded to Hector and stood back. Hector slid the key into the lock soundlessly and turned it ever so carefully. He swung the door open with his foot and we all looked inside. There was no activity in the front room, and the smell of cinnamon mixed with old lady perfume was stronger than the day I had visited with the flyer. We cautiously entered the apartment. The living room looked typical of any other living room: couch and loveseat with a decidedly old lady style pattern, a modest TV set, a couple of paintings on the walls. Nothing that suggested a monster resided somewhere inside. I also didn't see her dog anywhere. Charlie motioned to us to come in closer; we huddled up and came up with a plan for action. The door to the bedroom was closed; we figured that's where the "bug" was at. We told Hector to go first, since he had the gun, and Charlie and I would flank the door. We took up our positions and Hector put his hand on the doorknob. He turned the knob slowly and pushed the door open. This room was complete opposite of typical. There was no bedroom furniture and the window on the back wall was completely blacked out by a dark, shiny, mucus-like substance. There were what only could have been human bones strewn about the floor and there was a horrible smell emanating from the dark room. We didn't see the creature right away; it wasn't in our direct line of sight while we were all standing outside the room. Charlie nudged Hector gently towards the open door, he went in without protest. He looked to his left and didn't see anything and then he looked to his right and saw the abomination in the beam of the flashlight.

"*Madre de Dios*!" he exclaimed and raised the revolver at the creature. We entered the room right behind him and saw what Hector saw: the creature was sitting atop a pile of bones and was nibbling on the severed left arm of Charlie's date. The rest of her was on the floor, in a couple of pieces. The creature turned its remaining six eyes at us and roared, spewing bits of flesh as it did so. Hector panicked and fired off a shot, it struck the severed arm the creature was snacking on. It dropped the arm and hopped off the pile of bones, spilling them across the floor. It spread its four arms out and roared again, Hector took better aim this time and put a round in its abdomen. It yowled with pain and started across the room at Hector with that uncanny speed. It would've had Hector, too, but Charlie swung the bar with all his might and connected with the creature as it reached for Hector. Charlie caught the thing high in the chest area and sent it backwards on to the pile of bones. It stood up; there was a blue-green fluid oozing out of the hole that Hector had put in it with the revolver. It roared at us again and came at us; it was my turn this time to take a swing. I raised a ninja sword over my head and brought it down on the creature's cranium as it reached us. The blade struck the top of its head and stuck there, only going in a couple of inches, but it was enough to halt the creature's forward progress. It howled in pain again, and with two of its four arms it snapped the sword in half, leaving part of it protruding from its skull. Charlie raised the weight bar and thrust it at the creature, poking it in the chest and driving it back. Using all of his might he pushed it backwards and pinned it against the wall. I gripped my remaining sword with both hands and shouted at Hector to shoot it. He raised the revolver and tried to take steady aim, but was shaking too badly to accomplish this. I ran forward to join Charlie in holding the creature back; I stabbed at it with my remaining sword, but it kept swatting at it with the two arms that weren't preoccupied with the weight bar that Charlie had jammed into it. I finally got a clean shot at it and ran it through with my sword; the sword came out the back of the creature and embedded in the wall behind it. Hector finally managed to steady himself to aim the gun. He fired off two more shots; one struck the wall to the right side of the creature's head, the other one hit it in the mouth and exited the back of its head, leaving a blue-green and black spatter mark on the wall. Hector shouted in triumph and all the fight seemed to go out of the creature. I let go of my sword and Charlie gave one mighty final push of the weight bar against the thing. We both backed up and looked the creature over; I'm sure it would have slid down the wall had I not impaled it to it. Hector walked up to us and joined us in looking at the creature, gun still trained on it. More of the blue-green fluid was leaking out of its wounds, but there was no way we could determine if it was dead or not. As if to confirm our suspicions, the creature twitched against the wall and made guttural noises from its ruined mouth. Hector said something that sounded suspiciously like "Fuck this" and fired the two remaining rounds from his revolver. The rest of the creature's head was vaporized; black chunks and blue-green fluid went everywhere. It stopped moving and sagged against the wall. I removed my sword from the wall and the creature and it plopped to the floor. Charlie picked up his weight bar and poked at the thing a couple of times to assure himself the thing was dead. We exited the room and walked to the front door. I could hear sirens approaching; somebody must have called the cops after hearing all the gunshots. I didn't have the foggiest idea of what we were going to say to the police, but I didn't really care about that now. There were only two things on my mind: knowing I could now look at Krista without having the feeling I was letting her down, and that I was going to take the time to get to know my neighbors a lot better.

Hey, Me...It's Me Again

September 4th, 2014 had been a particularly uneventful day for Wendell Dane, up until he got the phone call. The phone call was notable because nobody ever called him. He kept the phone mainly for emergency purposes. He had a small circle of friends and there were his parents, but he just didn't like to talk on the phone. A quick text here or there was sufficient for him to get across whatever he needed to say. So when the phone's ringtone began it startled him a little. "I Wear My Sunglasses at Night" by Corey Hart issued forth from the phone; it had been so long since he last received a call that he had forgotten that that was what he'd chosen for his ringtone. He took the phone out of his pocket and looked at the display to see who was calling him. The number in the caller ID was his own. He pressed the connect button to answer the call.

"Hello? Who is this?" Wendell asked the phone quizzically.

"You."

"Come again?"

"I'm you, just 42 minutes behind you."

"I thought you sounded familiar."

"Hold on, I have to call you, me, right back." The line went dead and Wendell stared at the phone. It was silent for a minute and then it started up its ringtone again.

"Hello?"

"Hey, I'm now about 20 minutes ahead of you, in the future. I guess this will have to do."

"What will have to do?"

"The time frame. I have to be no more than an hour ahead of you or behind you in order to make a call. Don't ask me to explain it, I don't understand it myself. But there's no time for that right now. I have to warn you and the battery's almost dead. OK, real quick...WHOA! That was a close one!"

"What was a close one?" Wendell asked himself.

"Oh, it's the future; it doesn't like me being here. It keeps trying to kill me."

"Well that doesn't sound like much fun."

"Yeah, that time it was an open manhole, who knows what it will be ne—…" The call was abruptly terminated.

"Hello? Hello, are you there?" Wendell asked the silent phone. He took it away from his face and looked at the darkened display. As he looked at it, Corey Hart started to sing to him about wearing Ray-Bans in a nocturnal setting and the display lit up with his number again. He answered it immediately.

"Hello?"

"Hey me, it's me again. Sorry about that, the battery died out. I had to charge it for a couple of hours."

"A couple of hours? You were gone just a few seconds. I thought you got killed by the future or something." Wendell was confused. The Wendell on the other end of the phone didn't take notice. He actually sounded annoyed.

"Well, I had to find a charger or it would have been sooner. Keeping the phone plugged in to the device seems to drain the battery quicker and I forgot my charger."

"Wow, you must be using that thing a lot. I can go a week and a half without a charge and I've had this phone for three years with the original battery," Present Wendell stated.

"Yeah, it's mostly the device using the charge, it…oh, Jesus fuck we're babbling. Let's stay on task here." Future Wendell sounded even more annoyed.

"Sorry, sorry. Please, go on. You said you had to warn me about something?"

"Yes, right, but first things first. I need to explain how some of this works." Future Wendell took a big breath on the other end of the line and began. "OK, this is what I know. The present you leave from when you first use the device is the constant. Everything hinges on that. The past is cool; it doesn't mind you being there because it's already happened. You can go in there and dick around and change stuff and the past is all chill with it because it knows that the future will set everything right. For example, I went to the past to stop the JFK assassination, but you know what? It still happened after I left. It was still Lee Harvey Oswald, Kennedy was still shot in the head, and Jack Ruby still gunned down Oswald. And, best of all, Zapruder still filmed the assassination. It just shifted locations by a few miles and a few hours. The future makes stuff happen and the past is there to let you know what happened. But when you jump to the future from your current present, you're meddling with things that haven't happened yet. The future doesn't like this. An example of that would be when I went to 2018, and learned that aliens are real and will be living with us again very shortly. I come back to the present with that info and spread it around? That changes the future big time and REALLY pisses him off. Hence, the future always trying to kill me while I'm here."

"How do you know it's a 'him'?"

"Really? All of that and that's your question? Man, I used to be stupid."

"Well it is a lot of information to absorb. I didn't know where to begin." Wendell felt hurt that he would talk to himself this way. He began to ask a more meaningful question, but Future Wendell started talking before he was able to make his query.

"Moving on. I initially was going to warn you not to fuck with the device at all. But then I thought about it and realized that was no good, because you're me and I know I wouldn't be able to resist playing with the thing no matter who told me what about it."

"Wait, wait," Present Wendell said, cutting off Future Wendell. "If I go to the past and then back to the present, isn't that actually the future and he'd try to kill me?"

"Not if you return to the exact time you left, which is considered the established present. If I don't go any further past the time that I left, then I'm safe. But I've already destroyed that by going past the established present into the future. Now I just have to watch my ass."

"And that's what you're calling to warn me about?"

"Well, yes and no," Future Wendell said. "Partly yes, when and if, but mostly when, you come across the device, don't go to the future, past the established present. I'm quite sure you can have enough fun in the past. The other part of the warning is this, and you might want to write this down..."

"Hold on, let me get out a pen and something to write on," Present Wendell said, fumbling around in his pockets. He held the phone between his ear and his shoulder as he withdrew a pen from his left pants pocket and a scrap of paper from his wallet. "OK, go ahead."

"October 14th, 2020." A date. Present Wendell hastily scribbled it down.

"But wait, what good is that if I can't go to the future?" Present Wendell asked the phone.

"That's what I'm calling to warn you about. You need to make it to that date, alive. You have to live from your established present to that date. So, no fucking around in the future; if you do, you die." Present Wendell folded the scrap of paper and replaced it in his wallet.

"What's so important about that date?" Present Wendell asked.

"There's so much I can't tell you, but so much you need to know. I can't really tell you anything other than that date, stay alive and make it in one piece. There's someone you're going to meet that day that..."

The rest of whatever Future Wendell said was drowned out in the sound of an approaching car horn, starting out distant in the background, but growing louder as it neared the phone Future Wendell was speaking in to. Present Wendell stopped walking and listened as the horn drowned out whatever Future Wendell was trying to tell him and ended their conversation in a loud crash, followed by silence from the phone as the connection was broken. Present Wendell took the phone away from his ear and waited for Corey Hart to serenade him again, but it stayed silent. He began to walk slowly down the sidewalk, but was focused on his phone, waiting to see if his own number would display in the caller ID. The display stayed as dark as the phone was silent. Wendell then had the genius idea of trying the re-dial button, and pressed it. He listened as the phone dialed the number and connected. He put it to his ear excitedly. An ambulance screamed by him on the street, he took notice of it as his voicemail greeted him. He disconnected and watched as the meat wagon tore down the street and made a sharp right turn about a block down. Wendell pocketed his phone and started to jog down the sidewalk. The jog turned to a sprint when he was passed by another screaming ambulance, which made the same turn as its predecessor. He ran down the sidewalk towards the same intersection the ambulances had turned on and saw other people were running towards whatever calamity had occurred.

Wendell rounded the corner, following the cacophony of the sirens and the din of the ogling crowd. He saw the crowd of on-lookers all straining and craning their necks in attempts to get a better view and the emergency personnel buzzing about their business. He was unable to get a good look at what had happened from his current vantage point when he spied an area where not too many people were milling about. He sauntered over and got a good look at the horrific scene before him: a large sedan had jumped the sidewalk and completely obliterated some poor bastard all over (and into) the brick side of the building that the sidewalk ran parallel to. The driver of the sedan was unharmed; some little old lady who was shaken up and had momentarily confused the gas and the brake pedal. Wendell didn't really care about her, though, as his attention was focused on the victim of the accident. The features of the person were unrecognizable, having met the brick wall in a battle of strength, with said brick wall coming out on the winning end. Wendell didn't need to see the facial features of the person, however, as he was able to recognize his own favorite jacket. Wendell looked around and saw that just outside the circle of action that was the accident scene, laying in the gutter, was a phone similar to his own. He slowly made his way over to it, taking notice that no one was noticing him. He bent over deftly, picked it up, and slipped it inside his jacket. He stood up and made his way away from the crowd and any prying eyes. He ducked into an alley a block away from the accident scene and withdrew the device from his jacket for inspection. The phone was connected by a cord of some sort to what appeared to be a television remote control, but the kind of remote you could buy at a dollar store. Very cheap and very basic. It had number buttons on it, a forward arrow button, a back arrow button and a power button. There were a number of scuffs on the remote, as well as scorch marks, and where the cord was attached was done so with duct tape. Wendell pressed the power button and a green digital display lit up, much like the calculators he used in high school. Wendell pressed the number 8 key and filled the screen up with a row of 8's. It held enough numbers that Wendell surmised that it would hold the month, day and year, as well as the hour, minute and second. What he didn't know was which order to put them in. He pressed the power button and cleared the screen of the 8's then pressed it again to turn it back on. He punched in 12121212121212, meaning that the only destination he would go to would be December 12th of the year 1212, arriving at either 12:12.12 in the AM or PM. Holding his breath and hoping for the best, he punched the back arrow button.

Buzz

In the world of great office views, Janice Stampkeen had the tops. She could look out over the teeming city, with all the little office drones and worker bees flitting about and she felt like the queen of the ant-hill. Even when there was fog or low cloud cover she would look out her window and, though she couldn't see the ground, would still feel like the master of all she surveyed. The office itself was spacious and tidy, decorated in white and brightly lit. Janice was a big fan of crystals and along one wall was a collection of them lined up on shelves, with labels in front of them proclaiming their age and country of origin. She even had a couple of rare crystals that were collected from meteor crash sites that could only be from outer space. They had their own special area on the wall of shelves, and they were the pride of Janice's collection. There was not a speck of dirt on the floor, nor a drift of dust in the air: the office was cleaned twice daily, once in the hour before Janice arrived for the day and then once again after she was gone. Her desk was aimed at the large bay of windows that served as the outer wall of the office and on the wall opposite the crystal collection was a large digital television flanked by a pair of recessed bookshelves. One of the bookshelves housed a collection of books that had belonged to her father; the other held Janice's collection of vinyl records. The LP's had originally been her mother's, to which Janice had added to over the years. Underneath the TV, and in stark contrast to the modernity of it, was an old record player connected to unseen speakers. Along with the record collection, Janice had inherited her love of older music from her mother, often commenting on how much better music sounded when made by real instruments. She was currently listening to The Doors "Break on Through (To the Other Side)", the first song from their debut album released in 1967.

Janice was the CEO of a Fortune 500 company that her "dear departed" father had left her; truth be told she couldn't wait to get the old man in the ground fast enough. She'd have shot his ashes out of a canon if it meant getting the company faster. Though they were each other's only family since the elder Stampkeen had "accidently" killed his wife (Janice's mother) many years earlier, they were hardly what you would call close. Mr. Stampkeen, the old codger, always resented Janice for not being the "male heir" and Janice in turn resented the way her father treated her because of this. The mysterious circumstance of her mother's death was the icing on top of this particular hate cake. Mr. Stampkeen begrudgingly left the company to his daughter in his will; despite his feelings about her he would rather the company he built stay in family hands as opposed to greedy outsiders. Stampkeen Pesticides was the largest manufacturer of all purpose bug spray in the world, their scientists and researchers having unlocked a formula that would kill all bugs with just one can, as opposed to buying a separate can for flies, one for silverfish and roaches, yet another for spiders, etc. The formula even took care of bed bugs, one of the most notorious creepy crawlers in the insect kingdom, known for its ability to be as nearly as indestructible as Keith Richards. The wonder formula was also used on farms and in crop dusters, as it tested absolutely safe to humans and animals alike. Most recently the scientists and researchers were hard at work on an off-shoot of this formula that would be used as a bug repellant, making everyone's Fourth of July celebrations a little more mosquito free. Janice was currently having a heated discussion with the head of the project.

"Listen, you idiot, I'm not paying for excuses, I'm paying for results. All your blithering is saying is that you're not working hard enough. You need to be able to go to human trials by next week so we can be ready for the summer season. You need to figure out why it's killing the test animals and fix it." She slammed the phone receiver down as punctuation and fumed at her desk. The project was supposed to have been completed three weeks previous, and though the formula worked fine as a mosquito repellant, it also had the tendency to burn living flesh when applied.

She pushed back from her desk and stood up, pulling at the bottom of her suit jacket to straighten it. She clenched her hands tightly in to fists and then slowly released them. She grasped the large diamond ring on the middle finger of her right hand with her left and began rotating it slowly around her finger. Calm began to return to her and she let out a large breath. She took a seat behind her desk again, and the notes of "The Crystal Ship" played on. Her phone intercom beeped, her assistant was here with lunch. She entered the office with packages from Lucio's, and unbeknownst to her, she was not alone. A solitary common housefly had landed in her hair before she entered the building, and now inside the office, it took flight again.

The fly buzzed upward and landed on the ceiling, neither Janice nor her assistant had noticed it yet. The assistant set the packages from Lucio's on the desk momentarily and crossed the room to fetch a rolling service tray that was stashed in a corner. The tray was similar to ones used in fancy hotels for in room dining service: there was a metal box below the table that would keep the hot food warm until Janice was ready for it. The assistant set the hot food in this box and put a garden salad on the top of the table for the first course. She asked Janice if she needed anything else and when the reply was in the negative, she exited the room and closed the door behind her. Janice rotated her chair to face not only the tray, but the TV on the wall as well, to watch as she ate. The fly on the ceiling looked around, and immediately registered the presence of food in the room. It flew down from its perch on the ceiling and started to make passes around the room behind Janice. She heard it before she saw it, stopping mid-chew when she heard the buzz. She spun around, looking for the source of the sound, her temper almost red-lining. Of all the things man and beast in the world (as well as things inanimate), the thing she loathed the most was flies. And now there was one in her inner sanctum.

She stood up from her salad, determined to find the insect interloper. The fly, meanwhile, had keyed in on the source of the food and was lining up his tiny body to take a few passes at it, before settling in for a good meal. Janice looked around wildly trying to hone in on the source of the buzzing, and then finally located the fly as it circled her salad. She watched in horror as it descended on the food and lighted on it, making it forever unclean in her mind. She waved at the top of the salad to shoo the fly away and it indeed flew off, only to land on the salad once more. It moved this way and that on the lettuce leaves, looking for a place to start. Janice made an angry growling sound in her throat and took a more aggressive swipe at the fly on the salad and managed to knock the entire works on to the floor. This increased her already raised ire and she stomped over to the spilled salad and glared at it. She strode over to her phone and summoned her assistant to clean up the mess, which she did with haste as "Alabama Song" played on the record in the background, and Janice continued to hunt the fly. Janice told her assistant to fetch a can of bug spray and the assistant hurried out to do so. By the time her assistant made it back with the spray, it would be too late, but neither of them knew that.

Janice located the fly once more by following the sound of its buzzing and watched as it landed on her shelf of crystals. Janice sneered at it as it perused her prizes and made its way to where her special crystals were. The fly walked in and around them, much like a museum goer would stroll around looking at exhibits and paintings. Janice walked slowly over to the shelf to spy on her little intruder, but didn't dare swipe at it here for fear of upsetting her precious stones. She watched as the fly continued his journey around the crystals, unaware the she was spinning the diamond ring on her finger like mad. The fly stopped in front of one particularly beautiful crystal, one that looked like ebony stone on the inside but had a clear outer layer that pulsed color when struck with the right lighting. Janice kept a light trained on that one at all times, and the colors of the outer layer would swirl and change endlessly.

The fly jumped and landed on the crystal, and as it did, all the color stopped. As Janice watched, the color that had been pulsing through the crystal was now pulsing through the fly. It was also growing in size. Where it had been the size of a normal fly, it now resembled more of a large horsefly. The fly took off from the crystal and flew past Janice's face, using much larger wings and making a larger buzz. The crystal resumed its color pulses as soon as the fly had left it, but Janice hadn't noticed, as her eyes had followed the bloated fly as it sought out another meal, since its last one had been so rudely interrupted. The smells of the warm food in the hot box had permeated the office, and now the fly was in search of that. "Light My Fire" ended and "Back Door Man" began as the fly hovered over the service table. Janice retrieved a manila folder from the corner of her desk that contained some stock reports and took a few swipes at the fly as it made its trek around the room. Her hair had come loose from the bun she kept it in on top of her head, and she was starting to resemble a wild-woman as opposed to a top executive. She finally caught the fly broadside with the folder, felt it smack against its fat body and sent it careening. She offered a triumphant hoot and raced over to where the fly had landed to squash it under her foot. It flew off as she reached it, looking none the worse for wear, and bigger. It had now taken on the size of a large bumblebee.

Exasperated, Janice tried to come up with a plan while wondering where the hell her assistant was at with that bug spray. She decided to entice and entrap the fly with the rest of her lunch; it repulsed her to think of the fly on her food, but realized she could always get more food. She went to the hot box and pulled out the entrée, vegetable lasagna with extra ricotta, and placed it open on the service tray. She took the top of the to-go package and fanned the food, letting the smell drift in to the room. The fly keyed on it and flew directly towards it. It landed on top, the weight of it making prints in the melted cheese. It walked a few steps on the lasagna, inspecting it. While the fly was preoccupied with the lasagna, Janice sprang into action and slammed the lid of the to-go package on top, sealing the fly in. She would keep it there until her assistant got back, she thought, and would hose it down good with bug spray before replacing her food and getting back to the lunch she had been denied thus far.

Janice turned her back on the service tray with the trapped fly and looked aimlessly around the office. Behind her the fly buzzed inside the package, she could hear it bouncing of the sides of the container. She looked over her shoulder in time to see the lid to the container flip off, as the fly, now roughly the size of a dragonfly, escaped its prison. Jim Morrison and the boys were tip-toeing through "End of the Night" as the fly rose towards the ceiling and made a few figure eights around the room. It then settled on the TV screen, on which some FOX News talking head was bloviating. Janice huffed out an angry breath, and then screamed at the fly, a roar of pure rage. Her eyes briefly scanned her desk for something to throw; her temper demanded that she lash out. She settled on her computer keyboard, picking it up and violently ripping out the cords connecting it to the computer. She ran at the TV and swung the keyboard at the fly with an emphatic grunt. The keyboard embedded itself in the talking head's face, missing the fly by a mile, and with a few sparks the screen went dark. Janice looked around wildly and saw the fly circling the service tray, the lasagna not forgotten. It settled on the food once again and Janice huffed at it. Seeing nothing but red she charged at the service tray holding the food and the fly and tackled it like a linebacker would a quarterback and sent silverware, plate ware and lasagna everywhere. The fly had flown away, of course, still hungry and disappointed. It flew about the room for a minute and then settled on one of the windows that provided Janice with her excellent view. Janice, meanwhile, was busy collecting herself from the remains of the service tray and her lunch that was now a mess on the floor. She finally stood up and grasped the ring and began twisting it to calm herself. It spun around her finger lubricated by some of the sauce from the lasagna and she scanned the office with gritted teeth.

Janice saw the fly on the window; its head was pointed up, and it was busy cleaning itself. She crept up to the window slowly and straightened out her right hand. She turned the diamond ring on her middle finger so that the diamond was on the palm side of her hand. She stood stock still and with breath held, furious with anger. She pulled her hand and arm back ever so slowly, making it look as if she was saying "hi" to someone. The fly stayed where it was, looking larger than ever and still cleaning itself. The opening notes of "The End" had begun on the record, starting the final song of the album. Janice counted to three in her head and on the third count she swung her open hand at the window in a silent, graceful arc; meaning to smash that damn fly for good. Right before her hand made contact with the over-size fly, it flitted away. Her now single diamond encrusted palm struck the glass flat and shattered it, the glass falling outward and the force of the swing pitching Janice forward through the broken window. She had enough time to put both of her hands out to the side to catch herself, but both hands grabbed onto window panes full of broken glass and her weight and momentum were still carrying her forward. She struggled with all her might to pull herself back in the broken window, glass digging into her hands and slicing up her palms. She gritted her teeth against the pain and pulled backwards harder, making the mistake of looking down while she did so. It was clear enough to see the street below and to see that a commotion had already begun on the sidewalk over the falling broken glass. She could see the little ant-like people milling around and looking up; some of them pointing. The sight of it made her lose her breath and her grip on the broken window relaxed slightly. The wind that was blowing past the broken window she was hanging out of lessened to a breeze and everything became quiet. Just as Janice was about to make her final attempt to pull herself back in the window, she heard a low buzz begin behind her over the music. She couldn't see it and didn't dare turn her head, but knew what it was all the same. The fly was hovering over her desk in a lazy circle. After a few passes it flew directly towards the small of Janice's back. It covered the area with amazing speed and had enough force behind the impact to drive Janice the rest of the way out the window. She toppled out the window and started a head-over-heels cartwheel as she fell toward the pavement twenty stories down. She screamed until about halfway down, then ran out of breath and got confused and tried to scream and draw breath in at the same time. She was still trying to work this out when she impacted the pavement, bouncing back up a few feet and coming to rest on the sidewalk on a bed of broken glass that had previously been the window she used to so lovingly look out of. As she was laying there and the light was going out in her one remaining eye, she didn't feel any pain or have any fear. She had time left as her last breath was leaving her body to have one last thing fill her rapidly declining vision: it started as the tiniest of black dots until it filled the spectrum of her vision as the fly landed on her eye and began to look for something to eat.

213

21951081R00119

Printed in Great Britain
by Amazon